I0550601

Frederick Germaine
Presents

Eye Candy

A Romantic Love Novel

Also by Frederick Germaine

Ladies' Man: An Entertaining Love Novel

The characters and events in this book are fictitious. Any similarity to real persons, living or dead, is coincidental and not intended by the author.

Copyright © 2012 by Frederick Germaine
Published by: F. Germaine Publishing
Cover Design: Brand Concepts Creative Media
ISBN: 978-0-615-62375-7
Printed in the United States of America

Dedication

This book is dedicated to all the eye candy on planet Earth.

EYE CANDY

A ROMANTIC LOVE NOVEL

F. GERMAINE PUBLISHING
ATLANTA, GEORGIA

WWW.FREDERICKGERMAINE.COM

PROLOGUE

THE WEDDING IN HAWAII

SATURDAY, JUNE 30, 2007

The enchanting island coastline being that of Kauai, Hawaii, was more beautiful than I could have ever imagined. As I looked out the window of my resort bedroom, the thunderous waves from the Pacific Ocean bounced off the jagged rocks along the shore. Not far from there, the ever-so-white ivory sand extended throughout the coastline for miles. I was on the majestic island to marry the woman of my dreams named Monica Carmichael. Within a short period, she would soon be my wife.

"Are you ready to do this, Aaron?" I asked myself still looking aimlessly into the ocean. Before I could answer my own question, there was a knock at the front door.

"Hey, Aaron, are you ready yet?" said the noticeable voice from the door. "It's me, Sebastian."

Sebastian Carter was my best man for the small and intimate wedding ceremony on the island. He was a catch for every woman since he was tall, dark, and handsome. Other than that, we were best friends and co-workers at Donaldson and Bradshaw an architect firm back in Atlanta. There, we were both senior designers and loved our job. I met Sebastian when we were freshman at Florida State University. Back then, I was a geeky and shy eighteen-year old engineering major, and he was on his way to being named college football's freshman of the year by the Atlantic Coast Conference.

"Yeah, I'm in here," I shouted from my bedroom as I walked to the front door briskly in my boxers and tee shirt. "Just calm down and hold your horses."

As I opened the door, Sebastian stood there already in his tuxedo as if he was the one getting married.

"Aaron, you're not even in your tuxedo yet," he said entering my room.

"Relax Sebastian. I already took my shower and it's only going to take me fifteen minutes to get ready."

After I closed the door, we both walked promptly to my bedroom where I needed to finish getting dressed.

"Well, you better hope so because the ceremony starts in less than an hour. I already went down to beach and it's real plush and elegant."

"It should be. Monica's father spared no cost to see his only daughter get married the right way."

"With all that damn money he has stockpiled, I bet this wedding didn't set him back one bit. Come to think about it, I haven't seen the professor all day."

Before Sebastian could get the last statement out of his mouth, there was a loud banging knock at my door. We both knew it could only be one person with such a distinctive presence.

"Aaron, are you in there?" asked the firm voice on the other side of the door. "It's me, Dr. Carmichael."

"Well, speak of the devil," said Sebastian laughing a little.

"Quiet, Sebastian, before he hears you."

By now, I had my pants and shirt on and made my way to the front door for our visitor. Mister or should I say Dr. Carmichael was a tenured English professor at Emory University. He found it quite offensive if anyone called him anything else besides Dr. Carmichael. Outside of teaching at well-known Emory University, he was a New York Times Best-Selling author with a handful of published works. Lecturing and book tours kept him busy and also allowed him to amass a substantial amount of wealth from his recognition. The entire wedding, including everyone's first-class airfare and resort rooms, was paid by him.

"Hello, Dr. Carmichael," I said as I opened the door smiling.

"Aaron, I see you're not ready yet," he replied looking down at his watch while entering the room. "We have less than forty-five minutes before the wedding ceremony commences."

"Yes sir, I'll be ready shortly," I said closing the door behind him and tucking my shirt into my pants. "Plus, I have Sebastian here to make sure I look just right."

By now, Sebastian had made his way from the bedroom and joined Dr. Carmichael and I near the front door.

"Hello Dr. Carmichael," Sebastian said to the professor as he stood by my side. "You look very distinguished in your suit."

"Thank you, Sebastian," he said while tugging on the front portion of his suit that was already perfectly tailored. "Now Aaron, I just came by to wish you much success on the marriage to my daughter."

"Thank you, sir."

"Aaron, I know I don't have to tell you this, but I feel compelled to say it," began Dr. Carmichael with his short speech. "My daughter means the world to me and I want you to treat her with the utmost respect. Besides loving her with all your heart, I want you to remain faithful to her no matter what."

"Dr. Carmichael, I promise I wouldn't have it any other way for your daughter. I truly love her with all my heart and soul. Besides, I'm thirty years old and ready to settle down."

"That's good to hear, son. You know I've been married to my wife for over thirty years now and never once have I stepped out of bounds. I expect the same from you."

"I always promised myself if I ever got married, the one thing I would do was remain faithful. Dr. Carmichael, I have too much respect for your daughter to ever think otherwise."

"Just remember, Aaron, marriage is a work in progress. You only get out what you put into it. Nowadays, young couples want to rescind their marriage as soon as they hit a bump in the road."

I stood there nodding my head agreeing to everything Dr. Carmichael was saying. It all sounded good and I knew he meant well. Sebastian stood there in silence and listened also.

"Well enough of me babbling," he said finally coming to the end of his speech. "I'll let you finish getting dressed and see you in the wedding area shortly."

We shook hands, hugged each other, and then I opened the front door for his departure. The next time I would see him, he would be walking my bride-to-be down the aisle.

"Aaron, do you believe that crap Dr. Carmichael said about him never cheating on his wife?" Sebastian asked finally speaking.

"Why would he have to lie about that?"

"Oh, please! All married men cheat at some point in time during their marriage. It's just in a man's genetics."

"Well, Sebastian, you can exclude me from your all married men cheat theory because I plan on remaining faithful to my lovely wife. Plus, everyone is not trying to be a ladies' man and add another notch on their belt like you."

"Oh, so you got jokes."

"Come on now, you know I'm just kidding around. Besides, you and Shanna may even hit it off here at the wedding."

"Now, you really think you're a comedian today."

Shanna was Monica's close friend and designated maid-of-honor. The pair was very different as Monica was quiet and reserved while Shanna commanded attention and was a self-proclaimed know-it-all. The two hit it off at North Atlanta High School where they were teachers. Shanna couldn't stand Sebastian and the feelings were mutual with him too.

"Haven't you heard that opposites attract?" I asked placing my tie on.

"Never in a million years will me and her ever attract," he said. "And you can take that to the bank!"

Within a few minutes, I was fully dressed. Sebastian made sure there wasn't a glitch on my tuxedo and we made our way out of the room and down to the beach.

When the ceremony began, I couldn't have asked for anything else more picture perfect. The sun was setting in the evening sky as the burnt orange haze reflected off the blue ocean's waves. You could hear the sea in the near distance as a woman dressed in all white played soft music on a cello. The white gazebo, where we were to be married, was placed on the beach but far enough from the water to give the wedding a tranquil and romantic feel. The small wedding party stood near the gazebo, which was decorated in our color theme of white and coral.

Monica and I stood in the gazebo and faced the vast and ambiguous ocean. The ocean would symbolize no boundaries and our endless love for one another. To my right, stood Sebastian and of course Shanna was to my far left. In the center, facing the audience was Pastor McGregor, who would orchestrate the wedding. He was a dear friend of Dr. Carmichael and was elated to be presiding over the ceremony.

"Are you sure you want to go through this?" Sebastian asked in a whisper but loud enough over the music.

"Quiet," I mumbled barely moving my lips.

The music continued to play as we awaited instructions from Pastor McGregor. The eager onlookers included Dr. Carmichael, his wife Allison, a few colleagues from Emory, friends from his publishing company, and of course Monica's close friends. Missing from the audience were any members from my family. Since I grew up in foster homes my entire life, I really never had anyone I considered close to me.

"You may now face each other," ordered Pastor McGregor as the music came to a halt and he began to speak. "The book of Proverbs states, he who finds a wife finds a good thing, and obtains favor from the Lord."

As Pastor McGregor continued to speak, I barely heard a word he said. All I could do was aimlessly look into Monica's eyes knowing how she would complete me. She held my hand with a firm grip of nervousness and looked back at me as tears of joy slowly filled her eyes.

"Aaron, you may now recite your vows to your bride," said Pastor McGregor regaining my attentiveness.

Even though I had memorized and practiced my vows to Monica for what seemed to be a thousand times before the wedding, I felt a sense of nervousness come over me. Quickly, I regained my composure, took a deep breath, and began my recital.

"I Aaron take you, Monica, to be my wife, to have and to hold, from this day forward, for better, for worst, for richer, for poorer, in sickness and in health, to love and to cherish, till death do us part."

Streams of tears raced down Monica's face as I ended my vows. She took a quick second and slowly, yet carefully, wiped the tears from her face.

"Monica, you may now recite your vows to your groom," said Pastor McGregor after she had regained her composure.

As I had done, Monica said her vows effortlessly and with confidence. The ceremony was almost complete when Pastor McGregor spoke again.

"The wedding ring is a symbol of eternity," stated Pastor McGregor. "It is an outward sign of an inward and spiritual bond that unites two hearts in endless love. And now as a token of your love and of your deep desire to be forever united in heart and soul, you Aaron, may place the ring on the finger of your bride."

"Monica, I give you this ring as a symbol of my love and faithfulness to you," I said gently placing the shiny one carat diamond ring on her finger.

"By the same token, Monica" said Pastor McGregor again. "You may place the ring on the finger of your groom."

Monica did as instructed and Pastor McGregor spoke for the final time.

"By the powers vested in me, I now pronounce you husband and wife. Aaron, you may now kiss your bride."

The Fourth of July was only a few days away but I swore I heard fireworks over the ocean as I kissed Monica. While our lips were locked on each other, I didn't want that feeling to end. The woman on the cello began to play soft music again as the small crowd gave out a loud boisterous cheer and clapped continuously. Even Sebastian had vacated all doubt and joined in too.

"Monica, I love you so much," I said after we kissed momentarily and opened our eyes to each other.

"Oh, Aaron, I truly love you with all my heart."

Before she could say another word, I kissed her again but this time much longer. Today was the beginning, of the first day, of our lives together.

PART I

THE REVITALIZATION PROJECT

APRIL 2012: ATLANTA, GEORGIA

CHAPTER 1

The sweet aroma of hickory bacon filled the air and penetrated my nostrils. I stood in front of the dresser's mirror attempting to tie the perfect double Windsor knot getting ready for work. My meticulous attitude was the culprit as I was now on my third attempt dealing with my tie. As I gave a big sigh, I started the process again knowing I had to hurry as work awaited me this Monday morning. But more importantly, breakfast downstairs was just about ready.

Nothing much had changed in the nearly five years since Monica and I had been married. I still worked at Donaldson and Bradshaw as a senior designer and Monica also enjoyed teaching at North Atlanta High School. Well, I guess I did leave out one major change in our lives. Since the marriage, we had two bundles of joy named Brandon and Braylon. The twin boys would be celebrating their four-year old birthday next month. My wife and I would be celebrating our fifth-year anniversary the following month after that. Monica was responsible for putting the twin's birthday celebration together while I had to come up with a way for us to celebrate our anniversary. Currently, I didn't have a clue how I was going to put together the latter as I had to deal with the stress of a new project at work.

"Finally, now that's the perfect knot," I said to myself staring in the mirror. "You look like you're all ready for work."

I slipped on my burgundy loafers, grabbed my blazer, and retrieved my briefcase which was propped against the bed. The next stop for me was the kitchen.

"Daddy," yelled both boys, from the kitchen, by the time my shoes hit the bottom of the stairs.

Then without hesitation, they both rushed me with a hug as their mother looked on still preparing breakfast. Their mother had already dressed them.

"How are my two little munchkins?" I asked the boys welcoming each of them with a big hug while they both giggled and laughed.

"Daddy, are you going to work again today?" asked Brandon.

Brandon was born a few minutes before his younger brother Braylon and always took the leadership role when it came to questions or anything else. Braylon never seemed to mind either.

"Yeah, I have to," I said still holding the two. "I nominated myself the breadwinner for our family."

"What's a breadwinner?" he asked.

"Don't worry you're a long way from becoming one," I replied. "Let's go see what mommy is cooking in the kitchen this morning."

I left my blazer and briefcase next to the staircase. Then I grabbed the twins by their hands as we marched slowly forward.

"She's cooking meat," said Brandon once again taking the leadership role in the conversation.

The twins didn't know the difference between bacon, sausage, or ham. They did recognize the smell but referred to it all as meat.

"Good morning, sweetheart," I said to my wife before I kissed her on the lips.

"Morning, honey," she replied back after our lips departed. "So are you ready for the big day at work?"

"As ready as I'll ever be," I responded while sitting at the kitchen table with the twins joining me. "Mr. Bradshaw is finally announcing the full development plans for the revitalization project for the old General Motors assembly plant. Plus, he is going to reveal who will be the consultant assisting me on initial development designs."

After many lengthy months of bidding and negotiations, my firm was selected as redeveloping the now desolate General Motors assembly plant which had been closed down permanently a few years ago. The plant had become an eyesore which at one point employed thousands of workers. Now, the only thing that remained in the area was outdated machinery and forgotten memories. My firm would turn the area into a thriving mixed-use development consisting of high-rise condominiums, retail space, a nature park, and of course fine dining.

"Well, that's interesting," she said while placing the plates, silverware, and glasses on the kitchen table. "Hopefully he won't bump heads with you since you're so sensitive with your designs."

"Actually, the he is supposed to be a she according to the corporate grapevine."

"So there is no glass ceiling for women in Corporate America?"

"I presume not with Donaldson and Bradshaw."

"Mommy, I'm hungry," screamed Brandon from the table while his brother looked on.

"Okay, Brandon, the food is on its way," she reminded him.

By the time the hot food hit our plates, I licked my lips and realized how much I loved my wife. Even though the sex between us had diminished just a bit over the last few years, her great cooking was still consistent. Pancakes, bacon, sausage, and French toast adorned our plates. She even managed to dress the plates with a healthy course of sliced watermelon and pineapples.

Brandon was the first to dig into his plate after grace was said, while Braylon was a close second. As for me, I devoured my plate without haste. My wife looked on knowing the meal she prepared was pleasing to her family. Seasoning and spices makes food taste good but when you put love into the meal, like my wife did, it taste great.

"Honey, I'm wrecking my brain trying to decide on the twin's birthday event for next month," said my wife continuing our morning conversation. "I've narrowed it down to Six Flags, White Water, or a cookout birthday party at our house.

"Six Flags," yelled Brandon.

"White Water," shouted Braylon.

"See how difficult it can be," she announced.

"Well, I'll leave it up to you for the final and deciding vote," I said. "Besides, I have the harder task of planning our fifth-year anniversary event."

"So what do you have up your sleeve for our anniversary?"

"Now, that wouldn't be a surprise, would it?"

"Come on, Aaron, you're not even going to give me a hint?"

"Nope, not one."

It was now a few minutes after seven o'clock and my stomach was filled thanks to my wife. I wanted to arrive early enough at work well before my routine day which normally began around eight. Before I exited the table, I grabbed a slice of pineapple and stuffed it into my mouth.

"Alright boys it's time to go upstairs and brush your teeth," she said. "Then it's off to grandma's house."

Monica's mother was a stay-at-home mom for the majority of her marriage to Dr. Carmichael. Every weekday for almost the past four years, Monica would drive the twins from our Sandy Springs home to Dunwoody where the Carmichael's lived. Her mother was always overly anxious to see her grandkids and never minded her babysitting duties.

Monica would then make her way to North Atlanta High School to begin her day.

"Come on, Braylon, I'll race you upstairs," said Brandon to his younger brother as he removed himself from his chair.

"Okay," replied Braylon as he positioned himself in his sprinter pose.

Then without hesitating, the two boys flew upstairs with Brandon in the slight lead. Monica and I looked on as we thought how refreshing it would be to have so much energy.

"Good-bye sweetheart," I said as I leaned towards Monica giving her a kiss.

"Bye honey," she said back. "So what do you want for dinner tonight?"

"I don't know. Just surprise me."

"You mean like the surprise you have in store for our fifth-year anniversary."

"Exactly."

"Come on, Aaron, you're really serious about not giving me a little bit of a hint?"

"Nope, not one."

Before I stepped out of the front door, I ran upstairs to give the twins a good-bye kiss. I found them in their room debating over what shoes to wear. Quickly, I thought to myself, I wished my day was that easy. After I left their room, I made the trek downstairs and winked at my wife. Then I grabbed my blazer and briefcase and exited the front door.

Driving my Audi out of our gated community very slowly, I noticed my neighbor Mr. Newman who lived a few houses down. He was an elderly and eccentric man who was diminutive in stature. Around the same time each morning, he always walked his cocker spaniel he called, Jewels. There he stood on the sidewalk, outside his home, dressed in a blue robe with striped pajamas underneath them. On his feet was solid white bunny slippers that I always thought were only worn by women until I first saw him wearing them. Jewels was attached to a leash which I found comical because she couldn't have weighed more than five pounds or hurt a flea.

As the two made their way down the sidewalk, facing my vehicle, I lifted my left hand off the steering wheel and waved. Mr. Newman waved back, with a pleasant smile, while Jewels let out a wimpy bark as if she was trying to say hi. I chuckled a little and maneuvered my car out of the community.

Luckily for me, I worked just minutes from our house at the well known King and Queen Towers on Peachtree-

Dunwoody Road. The two thirty-four story iconic buildings towered over the North Atlanta skyline and could be seen from GA-400 and I-285 simultaneously. After traveling a short distance, I turned into the building's parking garage and found my reserved spot empty as usual. Once I parked my car in my designated area, I turned the vehicle off, and headed for the lobby's entrance.

CHAPTER 2

"Good morning, Mr. Malone."

"Good morning, Harold."

Harold was the building's shoe-shine attendant and had been for quite a while now. He was a proud black man who always wore slacks, a neatly pressed collared shirt with an apron over it, and of course well shined shoes. Shining shoes was his hobby that occupied his time after serving over forty-five years in the armed forces. His work area consisted of three steel chairs with brown leather seat cushions which were positioned on top of a solid oak boxed platform. He was the first person you saw as you entered the building.

"So, how are the wife and kids doing?" he asked causing me to pause in my stride towards the elevators.

"Everyone is wonderful. Thanks for asking."

"How about letting me put the perfect shine on those Allen Edmond loafers for you today?"

I looked down at my watch and noticed it was twenty minutes until eight o'clock and I still had plenty of time to make it upstairs. I also glanced at my new loafers he was referring to.

"It will only take five minutes," he said closing the sale. "And I'll make them shine just the way you like them."

"Okay, Harold, you've convinced me."

I took the middle seat while he carefully rolled up the bottom portion of my slacks, so they wouldn't get in the way of his polishing work. As I sat there, I noticed more people coming into the building. Even though he was an older gentleman, he had the memory of an elephant and remembered everyone's name he came in contact with.

"So are you ready for the big day?" he asked opening a can of burgundy polish.

"Yeah, I sure am."

Harold knew mostly everything that went on within the building and its tenants. He was sort of a grapevine of information with the majority of it being true.

"I heard your firm is revealing the plans for the revitalization project for the old General Motors assembly plant today," he said while lightly rubbing the polish on my shoes.

"That's right, Harold."

"Well, it's about time someone finally fixed up that area of town. Plus, it will bring in more jobs too."

"I couldn't have agreed with you more."

"I think that new consultant your firm brought in may also add a little spice to the project."

"Really?" I asked perking up a bit in my chair.

"Oh yeah, Mr. Malone, she is a real classy and confident woman. She's definitely some good eye candy to look at."

"So you saw her already?"

"Sure did. She came in about five minutes right before you entered the building all bright-eyed and bushy tailed."

"So how did you know who she was?"

"Come on now, Mr. Malone, I know everyone who walks through those front entrance doors. Besides, I overheard her asking the concierge what floor Donaldson and Bradshaw was on."

By now, Harold was putting the finishing touches on my shoes. He carefully rotated his shining towel over the bridge of my shoes making it pop like a miniature firecracker. He did this with precision as if he was still in the military.

"There you are, Mr. Malone. All shined up and ready to go."

I looked below to check out his work and found it to be impeccable as usual. By now, he was rolling down the bottom of my slacks.

"So how much do I owe you?" I asked while standing up still admiring my shoes.

"It's just five dollars for you, Mr. Malone."

I reached into my pants pocket and pulled out a ten-dollar bill. Then I gave it to Harold and continued my journey to the elevators.

"Thank you, Mr. Malone," he said with a large grin on his face. "Enjoy your day and give my love to your wife and kids."

"Will do," I replied back.

As I moved away from Harold's workstation, there were two gentlemen who walked up seeking to have their shoes shined. Before I arrived at the elevators, I noticed the sunlight beaming off my shoes from the building's skylight. It was positioned directly above the center of the lobby and always was an attraction to visitors who came into the building. Of course, the marble tiled floor beneath it received just as much attention too. I passed the friendly concierge and said good morning to her as always. She smiled at me, said good morning also, and then I got on the elevator with a group of people.

I finally made it to the thirty-second floor, where my firm was located, and proceeded out of the elevator. As I walked through the large double-glass doors, which had Donaldson and Bradshaw plastered on the front, I could feel the electricity in the air. The workers in the office were buzzed with energy and seemed a bit more lively than any other mundane Monday morning. As I made my way pass the desks of a few junior designers, I politely nodded and they returned the favor. My well shined loafers walked on the expensive dark tan carpet pointing in the direction to my corner office. I had traveled this route so many times I figured I could do it with a blindfold on by now.

When I reached my destination, there was Jane sitting at her desk which was just outside my office. She was staring at her computer screen as if she was reading something. Jane was like the grandmother I never really had. She was always smiling, neat in appearance, and had the solution to every problem that came up. She had been with the firm longer than I had been and garnered much respect from all the workers.

"Good morning, Mr. Malone. How was your weekend?"

"It was just fine, Jane. What about yours?"

"It was just grand," she said smiling as I stopped at her desk. "I had my grandchildren over the weekend while my daughter and son-in-law went to Gatlinburg for some time to themselves.

"Oh, really."

"Yes, we had a great time."

"So how old are your grandchildren now?"

"Well, Joey is six and Alana will be five later this year."

"My how time flies," I stated. "I remember it like yesterday when you were showing me their baby pictures."

"Yes, I do remember that too. By the way, I know your twins' birthday is coming up next month. Has your wife decided where their celebration will be?"

"She told me this morning it was Six Flags, White Water, or a traditional birthday party at our home."

"Well, those choices seem interesting enough."

"Yeah, the challenge is deciding on which one. Of course, Brandon wants to go to Six Flags and Braylon selected White Water."

"I see what you mean, Mr. Malone. Trying to get identical twins to agree on the same event can be challenging."

"So were there any messages for me early this morning?" I asked changing the subject back to work.

"Yes, as a matter of fact, there is just one," she replied. "Mr. Bradshaw sent out another message reiterating the meeting at eight-thirty in conference room A. He still plans on introducing the new consultant to all the senior designers and specific staff members regarding the revitalization project."

"Sounds great, Jane. Is there anything else?"

"Yes, but not pertaining to work. It has been a month since you last sent roses to your wife at North Atlanta High School. Would you like for me to send the customary red dozen to her today?"

"That would be perfect, Jane. I don't know what I would do without you."

I slightly turned my body and motioned to go to my office which was only a few feet away. Before I could, Jane interrupted me.

"Oh, Mr. Malone, there is one other thing I wanted to discuss with you."

"Yes," I said stopping in my tracks.

"I came up with a few ideas for you and your wife's fifth-year anniversary. I think you're going to like one of the concepts because it's different yet original."

"Jane, you're the greatest. Let's talk about it later."

She smiled and blushed all at once and went back to looking at her computer screen. Meanwhile, I entered my well-cleaned office and took a seat in my plush chair near the window. Outside my window, I saw traffic backed up for miles on I-285 which was normal in Atlanta. Before I could do anything else, in strolled my colleague, Sebastian.

"So, there is the man of the hour I've been looking for," he said calmly walking in and taking a seat on the edge of my desk.

"Well, now you've found him," I said in a confident way. "I assumed you received the notification about the eight-thirty meeting?"

"Yeah, I received the memo from Mr. Bradshaw already. Since we have a few minutes, let me tell you about my gorgeous date this past weekend."

"Come on, Sebastian," I said cutting him off. "When are you going to try and settle down?"

"When there are no more beautiful women in Atlanta," he said proudly. "Seriously, Aaron, maybe when I'm fifty years old."

"Fifty!"

"Okay, maybe forty-five. And speaking of beautiful women, the buzz around the office this morning is that the consultant Mr. Bradshaw hired for the revitalization project is a knockout."

"Yeah, that's what I heard already too."

"Well, that shouldn't matter to you one bit," he said standing up. "You're happily married, right?"

"That's right, Sebastian."

"Good," he said straightening up his tie. "That will leave more room for me to get better acquainted with her."

"There you go with your antics again."

"Anyway, Aaron, your plate is full even if you weren't happily married. You've been assigned one of the biggest projects in our firm's history, the twins' birthday is right around the corner, and your fifth-year anniversary is in two months."

"Exactly."

"Oh, come on Aaron, you're so close to mastering the five-year itch and you don't even know what to get your wife for the big anniversary."

"The five-year itch," I said inquisitively. "What's that?"

"They say if a married man can go the first five years of marriage without cheating, then he never will."

"Well, leave it to a single man to come up with something like that. So, what do you suggest I do for my wife on our fifth-year anniversary?"

Before Sebastian could give an answer to my question, the phone which sat on my desk disturbed our conversation. There was a sweet and kind voice on the intercom.

"Mr. Malone are you there?"

"Yes, Jane."

"I just wanted to inform you your eight thirty meeting starts in five minutes."

"Thanks, Jane. We are on the way out."

Sebastian and I put our manly conversation on hold as we made our way to conference room A. The conference room which could hold almost fifty people was located on the floor below us. We opted to take the stairs instead of dealing with the busy elevator.

When we arrived in the conference room, the place was buzzing with noise as everyone greeted their colleagues. I scanned the room which had a large rectangular cherry table placed in the middle of the floor. There were comfortable looking chairs on each side of the table as well. From the large windows, we had a panoramic view of Dunwoody, Sandy Springs, and even Alpharetta. Since the meeting was only for senior designers and upper management within the firm, there had to be at least thirty people already sitting at the table. We took our seat at the far end of the table. On the opposite end, at the head of the table, sat Mr. Bradshaw. To his right was his CFO, Mr. Black, and next to him was a very beautiful woman.

"Alright everyone," said Mr. Bradshaw in his distinctive voice standing up as the crowd went silent. "Let's begin the meeting since everyone is here now. As you all may know I'm Thomas Bradshaw the CEO and owner of this prestigious architect firm Donaldson and Bradshaw. Today, I'll be disclosing the full plans for the General Motors assembly plant revitalization project you all have been waiting for."

As Mr. Bradshaw gave his introduction speech, he naturally commanded attention. He was a very confident man yet brash when he had to be. Albeit, he received respect from everyone within the architect and financial world. This tall man with many years of experience and knowledge was dressed in a grey lightly-visible pin-striped suit which was obviously tailored-made. He even had the perfect color pocket square to accentuate his tie and shirt. He briefly talked about his humble beginnings and how his great-grandfather started the company on drive and determination after immigrating to the US from England in the nineteenth century. It was your classic rags-to-riches story which I had heard before but I listened with enthusiasm.

"Well, enough of my story and how the firm was started," he said. "Now the items you all have been waiting for. It gives me great pleasure to announce that Aaron Malone will be spearheading the revitalization project as the lead designer. Aaron, please stand up."

As I stood up, everyone in the room gave me a big congratulatory clap and it was well deserved. I had worked diligently since joining the firm and now all my hard work was paying off. As I smiled and raised my right hand as a gesture of thanks to the crowd they continued to clap. It seemed as if I had won some type of award or prize. After the clapping had ended, I took my seat.

Now ladies and gentleman," began Mr. Bradshaw still standing at the head of the table. "Please give a warm welcome to the consultant I have assigned to the revitalization project as well. I introduce to you, Ms. Tiffany Towns."

Right on cue, Tiffany stood up, smiled politely, and greeted the room full of eager on-lookers. The crowd's claps were almost noticeably louder than when I stood up. Her body was well-defined and chiseled. And on top of that, she was drop-dead gorgeous.

"Well, looks like you're going to have your hands full with that pretty young consultant," whispered Sebastian in my ear.

"Quiet Sebastian, let's hear what she has to say," I whispered back to him.

Mr. Bradshaw took his seat while Tiffany addressed the wondering crowd. She briefly explained her educational credits such as her undergraduate degree in engineering from Georgia Tech and a master's degree from Stanford propelled her consulting career. Her biggest achievement included consulting on the development of the Palm Islands in Dubai.

"Well-educated, experienced, and looks to kill for," whispered Sebastian in my ear again. "Hope you're not easily intimidated by all that talent and beauty rolled up into one."

"Not a chance," I quickly responded back to him. "Besides, it's not a competition, we're working together."

By the time Tiffany finished her speech the participants within the room were quite impressed. That's saying a lot since there were many designers with years of experience under their belts. Before she sat down, Mr. Bradshaw rose to his feet and thanked her. The crowd clapped again one final time. Then Mr. Bradshaw adjourned the meeting as he had a video conference scheduled from his office in a few minutes. He suggested to everyone that they take this opportunity to familiarize themselves with Tiffany. Mr. Black left right behind him.

Sebastian and I stood up as my colleagues came over and continued to congratulate me. Everyone else gravitated towards Tiffany. I decided to break away from my circle of friends and make a warm greeting to her. Nevertheless, before I could make a move, I noticed she had excused herself from the small crowd near her and was making her way over to me.

"Hello Aaron," said Tiffany with a million-dollar smile and extending her right hand to me.

"Hello Tiffany," I replied back shaking her soft hand. "It's finally a pleasure to meet you."

"Actually the pleasure is all mine, Aaron. I've heard so much about your work. Your reputation precedes you exceptionally well."

"Why thank you. Your credentials are quite impressive at the least. I look forward to our working relationship."

"As am I."

"Ummm," mumbled Sebastian as he motioned for me to introduce him.

"Oh, by the way, this is my good friend, Sebastian. He is one of the senior designers here at the firm."

"Nice to meet you, Sebastian," Tiffany casually said.

"Nice to meet you as well," exclaimed Sebastian as the two exchanged handshakes.

"So how are you transitioning back to Atlanta again?" I asked Tiffany turning the conversation towards us.

"Very slowly," she said. "So much has changed since my college days here. But, I still love Atlanta."

"So where are you staying?"

"I'm staying in temporary corporate housing at the Twelve Hotel in Atlantic Station."

"That's interesting."

"Yes, I know you were one of the contributing designers for the hotel."

"So, I see you've been doing your homework on my past achievements."

"It's always good to know who exactly you're working with," she stated in a bold tone. "I see you're married also."

"Happily married with kids," I said raising my left hand and looking at my wedding band.

"Well, you gentleman enjoy the rest of the day. I'm going to mingle a bit more with some of your colleagues."

Tiffany departed from us and formally introduced herself to a few senior designers waiting to speak with her. When she was out of our hearing range, I finally spoke to Sebastian.

"Harold was right. She definitely is some good eye candy to look at."

"I don't say this too often about beautiful women but I have a funny feeling about this one," Sebastian said looking at me squarely in the face.

"And what feeling is that, Sebastian?"

"It's called a man's instinct. Besides, you know what they say about eye candy, don't you?"

"No, what do they say?"

"Everything that glitters isn't gold."

CHAPTER 3

It was a few minutes after the noon hour and Monica was seated next to Shanna in the teacher's lounge at North Atlanta High School. The two had just initiated their forty-five-minute lunch. As Monica dug into her brown bag to pull out the chicken salad sandwich on rye bread she prepared earlier this morning, a voice came over the intercom system.

"Would Mrs. Malone please report to the front office as soon as possible," said the voice.

"Now, I wonder what Doris wants during our lunch break?" Monica said to Shanna.

"It must be important," said Shanna pouring ranch dressing over the Caesar salad that was in front of her. "You know Doris wouldn't call you unless it was."

Doris was the school's administrative assistant who handled important affairs. This included notifying teachers when they were immediately needed as Monica was now.

"Well, I'll be back in a minute," said Monica standing on her feet.

"Okay, I'll see you when you get back."

As Monica made her way to the front office, she wondered why she was needed. First, she thought about her twins and hoped everything was alright with them. Secondly, Aaron came to mind. As the anxiety built up, she quickly moved faster to her destination. Making her way down a corridor and through a set of stairs she finally had her eyes fixed on the school's front office. She took a deep breath and turned the door knob.

"Hi Doris," said Monica entering the office with a set of mixed emotions. "I heard your announcement over the intercom. Is everything alright?"

"Yes, dear, everything is alright," replied Doris standing behind the chest-level counter. "I thought you'd like your gift now instead of later."

"What gift?"

"These beautiful dozen red roses that were just delivered here for you a few minutes ago," Doris said pointing to the far end of the counter.

The full bloom red roses were elegantly positioned in a glass vase and even added atmosphere to the school's office. They sat there waiting for Monica to pick them up.

"Oh, my, they are beautiful!"

"Yes and there is a card attached to them also."

"I wonder who sent these to me."

"I think you know but read the card just to be sure."

Monica quickly reached within the vase and pulled the small white envelope out. She opened it and found a tiny card which had a brief message on it.

"Well, Monica, what does it say?"

Monica stood there speechless, smiling, and teary eyed. Finally, she answered Doris' question.

"The roses are from my husband, Aaron. He wrote: *Roses are continually red as my love is for you. I want to spend the rest of my life, plus eternity, forever loving you. Love, Aaron.*"

"Oh, how sweet, Monica. You're so lucky to have a loving husband like Aaron."

"Yes, he is a great husband and father."

Monica carefully picked up the vase of roses and made her way back to the teacher's lounge where Shanna was waiting. A few more teachers had arrived in the lounge since her brief departure. All eyes gravitated to the display of roses she was carrying as she walked over to her table.

"Well, let me guess who sent you those lovely roses," said Shanna with an inquisitive stare.

"Yes, Shanna, you already know they are from Aaron," Monica said carefully placing the roses on the table and taking her seat.

"When am I going to find a man to love me as much as Aaron loves you?"

"Patience is a virtue, Shanna."

Monica finally took a bite out of her sandwich but could hardly take another one due to all the excitement with the roses. Shanna read the card that Aaron had sent and smiled while a few of the teachers came over admiring the roses.

"I must say, Aaron has a flair for being a romantic husband," said Shanna still looking at the roses. "I know who is in store for some good loving tonight."

"And you know I'm a hopeless romantic too."

"With the twins upcoming birthday, his rigors at work, and your anniversary coming soon he still found time to send roses."

"Tell me about it. I can barely get the plans together for the twins' birthday."

"So how are the plans coming along anyway?" Shanna asked.

"I've narrowed it down to Six Flags, White Water, or a birthday celebration at our home."

"Well, don't let it wreck your brain whatever you decide the twins will enjoy it. So what are your plans for the big wedding anniversary?"

"I don't have the slightest clue," said Monica tiding up their area on the table as their lunch break was almost over. "Aaron is in charge of that since I'm responsible for the twins' birthday."

"Judging by his romantic taste, I'd say you won't be disappointed."

The two women said their good-byes as Monica made her way to her senior English class while Shanna would teach the biology class she really loved. Monica was so excited about the roses Aaron sent her, she couldn't decide on which new Victoria Secret outfit to put on for him tonight. Either way, she was definitely going to show him her gratitude.

As Monica reached her classroom, there were a few students trickling in behind her. She placed the ever-so-beautiful roses on her desk which faced outwards towards the students. Then the bell rung which meant it was time for the class to begin. Before speaking, she overlooked the class and made sure everyone was in their designated seats.

"Okay class let's begin where we left off on Friday," she announced. "Who can compare and contrast one irony element in Shakespeare's novels 'Macbeth' and 'Anthony and Cleopatra'?"

"Oh, Mrs. Malone," said a student from the front of the room raising her hand. "I can."

"Yes, Marilyn, let's hear your answer."

Marilyn was one of the brightest students in Monica's class and the entire school. She already accepted a full academic scholarship to Vanderbilt University. There she planned to major in English and become a professor.

"Sure, but first may I ask who brought you those lovely roses?"

"My husband. Now your answer."

"Well, I would buy roses for you too if you were my beautiful wife," cried out a male student from the back.

"Danny!" shouted out Monica giving the student a scornful look while the class erupted in laughter.

As you may have guessed, Danny was voted senior class clown and liked by everyone. He had a way with one-liners and smart aleck responses. Surprisingly, he excelled in academics too and received a full scholarship to Wake Forest University where he planned to major in law.

"Sorry, Mrs. Malone, for the outburst," he said with a sly grin on his face.

"You may proceed with your answer, Marilyn, before you were so rudely interrupted," said Monica while still giving Danny a stern look.

As the class listened, Marilyn answered Monica's question more in depth than she had anticipated. For the remainder of the eighty-minute class, the students carried on an intriguing conversation about Shakespeare and his many works. Then the bell rung and the next group of senior English students walked in.

At precisely three-fifteen the final bell rang for the day. Monica decided to leave the roses on her desk so she would have something beautiful to look at throughout the remainder of the week. She eagerly walked to the parking lot, jumped in her Chevy Tahoe and headed to Dunwoody for the twins. She couldn't wait to give them a hug and a kiss. More importantly, she couldn't wait for what was in store for her and Aaron later that night.

CHAPTER 4

It was almost seven-thirty when I finally arrived home. I pulled my car into the garage after one of the most exciting yet busy days at work. As I entered the home, our alarm system chimed as usual. It was a way to let the occupants know someone had just entered.

"Daddy's home," I shouted out to anyone who would be listening.

"Daddy, daddy," screamed the twins running towards me from around the corner.

"Hey boys," I said smiling as I scooped both of them up in my arms. "So how was your day?"

"We had fun at grandma's house, daddy," blurted out Brandon clinching onto a cartoon action figure in his hand.

"Yeah, and look what mommy bought us," said Braylon holding up his cartoon action figure. "We got it in our happy meal from McDonald's after we left grandma's house."

"Well, good for you two," I said. "Looks like you can add those to your ever-growing collection. So where is mommy now?"

The question I asked was really a moot point as the scent of pot roast savored in mushroom gravy, red potatoes, and bell peppers with onions resonated throughout the house. It was also the first thing I smelled when I entered the home.

"She's in the kitchen, daddy," answered Brandon before his brother could get a word out. "Do you want to watch the movie with us?"

"What movie is that, Brandon?"

"*Happy Feet Two*," he exclaimed in joy

"Mommy bought us the DVD today after we left McDonald's," uttered Braylon still holding up his cartoon action figure.

"Well, maybe later I'll watch the movie with you two. Let me go and see what mommy is up to in the kitchen."

"Okay, daddy," said Brandon. "Come on Braylon lets go finish watching the movie."

Without hesitation, Braylon complied with Brandon wishes. They both ran into the living room like two little cheetahs and disappeared right before my eyes. I shook my head and smiled, then made my way to the kitchen to see my wife.

"Hi, sweetheart," I said entering the kitchen.

"Hello, honey," she said wrapping her arms around my neck and giving me a kiss. "I'm so glad you finally made it home."

Monica was still dressed in her attire from work and looked sexier than ever. She wore a nice pink-printed dress that showed a little bit of her cleavage. Along her neck and arms were the right accessories to give her dress a bit of flair but remain conservative too. Her waistline showed the perfect figure which no one would ever imagine she had twins.

"I'm glad to be here."

"Thank you so much for the roses, honey. You really know how to brighten up my day, especially since the school year is coming to an end."

"A lovely lady should always have lovely roses," I said taking the dinner plates out of the cabinet in an attempt to set the table. By now, I was thinking how lucky I was to have Jane as my secretary.

"So how was your day at work with the new consultant?" she asked still smiling at my last comment.

"It was good. Tiffany, that's her name, seemed to be a very likable and knowledgeable candidate whom Mr. Bradshaw selected. She even completed her undergraduate degree here in Atlanta."

"Oh really. Where?"

"Not too far from here over at Georgia Tech with a degree in electrical engineering. She even finished top of her class and then went to Stanford for her masters."

"Interesting, I'm so glad to see Mr. Bradshaw being open-minded and having a well-qualified female to assist you on the redevelopment project."

"Yes, but beginning tomorrow I'll have my work cut out for me," I said continuing to set the table. "Today, Mr. Bradshaw officially assigned the redevelopment project to me which has time-sensitive deadlines. That means a lot of late hours at the office and proof presentations for his approval."

"Well, the boys and I understand, Aaron. Besides, once you do come home, I'll be able to relieve you from your hard day at work."

"So what did you have in mind?" I asked prying into her imagination but knowing where she was going with the conversation.

"For starters, we can begin tonight with playing dress up. I'll be the naughty school girl and you can play the big, bad, and mean principal."

"Oh, I like that! However, you know what happened last time you played that roll. We almost woke the kids."

"Yes, I remember," she said chuckling. "But they should be dead asleep in a few hours. I took them to their favorite park earlier where they played and ran their little hearts out. Thus, they'll be fully knocked out after their bellies are full."

"I could always leave it up to you to come up with a master plan like that," I said pulling a chair out from the table. "Come on boys, dinner is ready. It's time to eat and then it's off to bed."

When the boys eagerly entered the kitchen, we all sat down. Then I led grace and we dug into the pot roast.

"Well boys, I've finally decided how we are going to spend your fourth birthday celebration," Monica said sitting from table without having touched her food.

"Mommy, I want to go to Six Flags and I mean it," Brandon said in a loud voice.

"No, no, no Brandon," yelled Braylon with his mouth partially full. "It's going to be White Water."

I dug in further to my pot roast and simply looked down at my plate. I knew Monica had her hands full trying to select the birthday event and I didn't want any part of it.

"No, we're not doing either one of those this year," she said in a stern voice even catching my attention. "Instead, we are going to have the biggest birthday party right here at the house with all your friends and family."

"Mommy, I don't want to do that," said Brandon pouting with fake tears in his eyes.

"Well, just wait a minute and hear me out," she continued. "With the birthday party, all your friends can come over and bring you lots of gifts and toys. Plus, we can have a bouncy house of your favorite cartoon character with grandpa cooking burgers, hot dogs, and barbeque chicken on the grill."

Once the boys' brains comprehended all the gifts and toys they stood to take in, their eyes lit up. Between the neighbors, our friends, and co-workers kids there were surely to be at least fifty kids at the birthday party. I didn't have any complaints because at the end of the day it would be well worth it.

"Yeah, presents and toys!" screamed the two together.

"Sounds like a great idea, Monica," I said as I paused long enough to take a break from eating. "The idea of your dad on the barbeque grill is a must-see."

"Come on, Aaron, you know my dad is a self-proclaimed chef. I would be remised, and he offended, if I didn't delegate him as the cook on that day."

"I agree."

After we all completed our dinner, it was time to put the twins to bed and spend some quality time with my wife. Monica stayed downstairs in the kitchen and washed the dishes while I tended to the boys and made them take a hot bath. They enjoyed their bath but even more so by playing with the cartoon action figures from earlier. That being said, it was a challenge trying to get them to remain still and clean them. Finally, after about twenty minutes struggling in the bathtub the boys were clean as ever. I toweled them dry and put on their matching Batman pajamas.

"Okay, guys it's time to hit the sack," I said as we all stood in their room. "Give me a kiss and climb into your beds."

I noticed Braylon yawning as he climbed into his twin-size bed. Quickly, I thought about how Monica's sediments were so right and her master plan was in full effect now.

"Where's mommy?" asked Brandon reluctantly climbing into his bed after giving me a kiss.

"She'll be up in a minute and give you two your goodnight kiss. For now, it's lights out."

I tucked Brandon in pulling the top sheet and blanket up to his shoulders. His eyes were heavy with sleep as if the Sandman had just arrived. Then, I turned toward his brother's bed and pulled up his covers making sure he was secured and comfortable. Not to my surprise, he was already dead asleep. I kissed him on his forehead then exited the room but leaving their door barely open. The night light in their room illuminated it just enough so you could see they were both asleep from the hall.

As I looked farther down the hall, I noticed our bedroom door was ajar and I could hear the shower running. There was a slight bit of steam slowly making its way out of the room. I knew Monica was unwinding with a boiling hot shower which she always loved to do. That was my cue to go downstairs and retrieve two small glasses of wine. Once I made it back upstairs, all the lights in the bedroom were off and few scented candles were burning. The radio was playing nothing but pillow talk music.

"Well, Mr. Principal, I see you finally made it," said a voice from behind me as I walked into the bedroom.

When I turned around, it was Monica all dressed up in her naughty Catholic school girl uniform. Her skirt was royal blue and made extra short which showed her sexy legs and thighs. Of course, the matching top was even sexier and was super tight hugging her breasts which were in a Victoria Secret bra.

"What took you so long?" she asked.

"Well, I had to go downstairs and…"

"No talking now," she said taking the glass of wine from my hand. Then she walked around me in a circular motion very slowly while touching me with a small leather whip. "You know, Mr. Principal, I've been a very naughty girl today."

"So you know what that means," I said still looking forward as she circled back into my view. I took a brief moment and took a small sip of the wine from my glass.

"Punishment I assume."

"You're damn right."

"Are you going to give me a demerit, Mr. Principal?"

"No."

"What about putting me into school detention?"

"No."

"So what are you going to do to me, Mr. Principal?"

"I'm going to give you a good spanking you deserve."

Now some married couples going on their fifth year of marriage lived a bland one. The ups and downs of marriage can do that sometimes. Even so, not Monica and I as we always used creative role playing as a prelude to love making which helped break the monotony of just sex.

We both put our glasses down after finishing off the remaining wine that was in the bottom of it. Then, I grabbed the small, yet soft, leather whip out of Monica's hand and pushed her on the bed. She lay on the bed with her backside facing me.

"Now turn over on your back," I ordered after I struck her naked rear end a few times.

"Oh, Mr. Principal, I'm so ready for the rest of my punishment," she yelled out.

Then like a male virgin on prom night, I dove in face first as Monica spread her legs wide open. I gave her a slow, gentle, and relaxing massage on her clitoris with my tongue that made her shiver. For the next fifteen minutes, I kept my face buried in between her legs while she moaned.

"Aaron, baby, I'm almost there!"

"No, you don't, what's my name?" I asked pausing for a minute coming up for air.

"I mean, Mr. Principal. Don't stop go back down!"

As she commanded, I obeyed like a good husband watching her erupt like a volcano. My tongue never missed a stroke as I looked at my wife's face which was extended to the ceiling as her back arched. Violently, her legs trembled as she squeezed her legs around my head but I kept stroking with my tongue. When her episode was over, I licked the flowing juices not letting a drop waste. Then, I climbed on top and we both came together. After our gratifying efforts, we both fell sound asleep. She even forgot to give the twins their goodnight kiss.

CHAPTER 5

The elevator doors briskly opened and I made my way into the office for another day at Donaldson and Bradshaw. As I pushed opened the large glass doors, I noticed the hustle and bustle of the firm seemed to never stop. It was only seven-thirty and everyone was busy or seemed to play the part very well. I began my normal trek to my corner office as I did so for so many years. But on this particular morning, it was different. Today was the official day I began working on the revitalization project so I walked with more pride.

"Good morning, Mr. Malone," said a young man pushing a stainless steel cart full of mail.

"Good morning, Ryan."

Ryan was our head mail room clerk who had been with the firm for a few years now. Everyone liked him because he was smart, efficient, and most importantly never screwed up the outgoing mail. He had aspirations of being a celebrity trial lawyer like his idol, Robert Shapiro, who resided in Los Angeles. A pre-law major at Mercer University, often Ryan could be caught watching the latest segment of *Court TV* in any one of the company's three break rooms during his lunch.

"Good morning, sir," said a young pretty woman walking past me as I came even closer to my office.

"Good morning to you," I replied back.

I had never seen her before and figured she was just another temp the company had hired. Mr. Bradshaw was well-known for that as it saved him more money not paying high salaries and benefits.

After walking through the office maze, I was almost at my destination. I noticed in the short distance ahead of me stood Sebastian and Tiffany having a candid conversation at the water cooler right outside my office door. I figured Sebastian was up to his old tricks again and taking a stab at getting to know the new consultant. Mr. Ladies' Man had every intention of seeing if he could land her in the sack as he did with every attractive woman who came into our office.

I shook my head and smiled, thinking I guess you just can't teach an old dog a new trick. Surprisingly, their conversation seemed to be going well as Tiffany's body language was very receptive to whatever he was saying to her. Within a few seconds, I finally walked up to the pair.

"Well, if it isn't the man of the hour once again," Sebastian said turning his head away from Tiffany and her smile.

"Good morning, you two," I said quickly trying to get to my office. "I hope I wasn't interrupting anything."

"Actually no, Aaron," Tiffany said. "We were just talking about how everyone is excited to see the initial sketches for the revitalization project."

"Yes, this is one of my biggest projects ever, but I think you'll be quite impressed," I said boastfully. "Now, if you two will excuse me, I have a one-on-one meeting with Mr. Bradshaw I'm on my way to."

"You mean the meeting at seven forty-five?" asked Tiffany.

"Yes."

"Well, Aaron, I'll be joining you two for the meeting," Tiffany said smiling even more by now.

"You will?" I asked in an astonished tone. "I didn't get word of that in my memo yesterday."

"Mr. Bradshaw's secretary just sent me an email notification right before I arrived here at your office today," Tiffany calmly said. "Don't worry, Aaron, I promise to be all ears and won't get in the way."

"Mr. Bradshaw probably overlooked the technicality yesterday in the memo to you, Aaron," said Sebastian finally breaking his silence. "You know how he can be since he is so busy and all."

"Well, who am I to question the man who signs the checks, right?" I asked. "Besides, it will be good for you to sit in with us. The left hand always needs to know what the right one is doing so they're on the same page."

"I couldn't have agreed with you more," Tiffany said. "So are you ready to proceed to Mr. Bradshaw's office?"

"Sure."

"I'll catch up with you later, Aaron," said Sebastian after drinking the remaining contents from his cup.

"Sounds like a plan, Sebastian," I replied back.

"And enjoy the rest of your day and stay here, Tiffany," Sebastian said with a gentlemanly smile throwing his paper cup in the trash can next to the cooler.

"Why thank you," she exclaimed. "And you do the same."

As Sebastian walked away, Tiffany and I strolled towards Mr. Bradshaw's office. It was on the same floor but completely on the other side. His office nearly dwarfs the size of mine and almost took up one-half of the entire floor. From his office, one could also see the beautiful and breathtaking views of the North Georgia Mountains.

When we arrived in front of Mr. Bradshaw's office, his secretary desk was right outside his door. She kindly motioned us to enter as she knew we were expected. There were two giant oak-colored doors that stood side by side leading into his office. They both extended from the floor all the way to the ceiling. I grabbed the shiny brass handle to one of the doors and opened it inwards for Tiffany. Then, I motioned for her to enter first. I followed behind her, closing the door after me.

"I see you two have arrived," said Mr. Bradshaw sitting behind his enormous cherry-colored desk. "Please, come in and take a seat so that we may begin."

I had only been in his office a few times, but every trip seemed so intriguing. Behind him was the majestic view and his office was well kept and clean. We took our seats in two separate chairs right in front of his desk. He was rumored to have over a thousand tailored suits and on this particular morning he was wearing one of them.

"Aaron, I just wanted to say once again, we are so proud to have such a seasoned designer leading the revitalization project."

"Thank you very much, sir."

"As you may have imagined, the project will serve as a stepping stone for major ones to come from this firm," he said crossing his arms and leaning forward in his chair. "Thus, it is very imperative the development goes on without a hitch. Anything short of perfection would simply be a failure."

For the next thirty minutes or so, we listened to him adamantly while he discussed details, expectations, deadlines, and budget constraints. He didn't mind mentioning how successful he anticipated the project would be. The first deadline included having the initial proof designs of the project to him within seventy-two hours. Additionally, we all were to meet at the General Motors assembly plant location one week from this Friday. At the meeting would be engineers, project managers, upper management from Tiffany's consulting firm, and the ever-important investors. The purpose of the on-site meeting was to present the initial designs to the individuals outside the firm involved on the project.

When the meeting ended, we made our way out of Mr. Bradshaw's office. As Tiffany predicted, she hardly said one word while the meeting was being conducted. Excited, I raced backed to my office and she followed right next to me.

"I think that went very well," she said keeping up with my hurried pace. "Seems like Mr. Bradshaw knows what he wants and how to go about getting it."

"It's just how one of the richest men in the city operates," I said. "Today, you received an up close and personal view. Welcome to Donaldson and Bradshaw."

By the time we approached my office, there was Jane pecking away at the computer which was on her desk. As normal, she noticed us in her peripheral vision and paused for a moment.

"Good morning, Mr. Malone," she said in her forever kind and friendly way.

"Morning, Jane," I said quickly knowing I didn't want to be bothered with any small talk.

"Good morning to you as well, Ms. Towns," Jane said holding her perfect smile. "I see you're getting better acquainted with Mr. Malone."

"Yes I am," replied Tiffany. "He's quite the man around here. Now, if I could only see the inside of his office and how the mad scientist operates."

"You know you're more than welcome inside my office," I said standing outside my office door. "Besides, we're partners for a short while."

I led Tiffany into the area where all the creative ideas were born. As I looked back and closed the door behind us, Jane went back to working at her computer again. I offered Tiffany a seat but she remained standing looking throughout my office décor. She finally walked up to my college diploma that was framed on the wall near my desk.

"So, I see you're a Florida State graduate," she said placing her hands on her hips with her back towards me.

"Yeah, actually Sebastian and I are the only FSU alumni who work for this firm."

"So how did you and Sebastian meet at Florida State?"

"It had to be all sheer luck," I said while looking at the diploma and reminiscencing. "Apparently, through a computer error, I was assigned to a luxury off-campus apartment unit that housed the student athletes. Sebastian, who was a standout football player, was my first roommate during our freshman year and we had been friends ever since."

"Interesting," she said moving away from the diploma and slowly looking at my achievements and awards that adorned the wall.

"Yeah, tell me about it," I said taking off my jacket and positioning myself at the workstation away from my desk. "He could have easily reported the mishap but instead we kept it our little secret. Eventually, he got me tickets to all the sold out home football games even when our rivals, the Miami Hurricanes, came to town.

"It seems like Sebastian is popular with the ladies, here in the office, as I imagined he was on campus."

"I see you've taken notice during your short time here"

"I have but I'm not interested in his type."

"Well, Tiffany, I have a lot of work to do and it starts with the initial sketch designs that are due shortly to Mr. Bradshaw," I said while rolling up my sleeves at my workstation and taking a seat. "I'm sure you'll excuse me now."

"I understand, Aaron," she said looking at me in an untruthful way. "But be careful about working too hard."

"Why is that?"

"Because all work and no play makes Jack a very dull boy."

Tiffany turned around and walked to my office door and let herself out. I sat there with a perplexed look on my face not knowing whether to laugh or comment before she departed. For that moment, I realized the revitalization project was big but maybe dealing with Tiffany was going to be my biggest project ever.

CHAPTER 6

The weekend had arrived and it was well worth the long wait. I had managed to deliver the initial prints to Mr. Bradshaw and had received his seal of approval. Even Tiffany complimented me on the futuristic outlays and how realistic the approach seemed to be. I shouldn't have taken all the credit because the designer software system I used helped out tremendously. Now, I just had the presentation to deal with next week. However, right now that seemed too far away to think about.

On this particular Saturday, we decided to take the twins to the Atlanta Zoo. They had never seen real animals up close and personal but today they would be in for a real treat. We contemplated about going to Six Flags but the weather in Atlanta was still a little breezy on this late April Saturday. And going to White Water was definitely out of the question.

"Daddy, are we going to see Barney at the zoo today?" asked Brandon.

"No, Brandon," I said answering his funny question. "Barney is only a cartoon character on television. We are going to see real-live animals today."

I had my hands full again getting the twins dressed while attempting to answer their eager questions. I managed to coordinate their matching outfits to include blue jeans, Atlanta Braves tee shirts, and a pair of grey Nike sneakers. Besides them looking like identical twins, they would be comfortably dressed also. While I conquered the challenge of dressing the two, Monica was busy downstairs preparing breakfast.

"Yeah, Brandon like the ones we watch on the Animal Planet channel at grandma's house," blurted out Braylon as I tugged his tee shirt over his head.

"That's right Braylon," I said. "So, I see grandma is making you learn about animals."

"Yes," Brandon announced as he looked confused trying to tie the shoestrings on his sneakers. "She said we needed to learn all the animals in the world before we go to school."

"Yeah, your grandma has a great point there. So what animals do you boys know now?"

"We know about elephants, lions, and bears," yelled out Braylon.

"And rhinoceros, zebras, and giraffes," followed up Brandon as he didn't want to let his younger brother outsmart him.

After our brief lesson in zoology, the twins were finally fully dressed. As they stood side by side, I could only tell them apart because I was their father. Anybody else would have the ultimate challenge on their hands today.

"So are you two ready for the zoo today?" I asked in an exuberant tone.

"Yes!" they both responded jumping up and down while clapping their hands.

"Okay, let's go downstairs and see what mommy has in store for us," I shouted back while they still cheered.

Traveling downstairs the scent of ham and cheese omelets, hash browns, and grits suffocated our noses. Brandon was so excited he pulled away from me to get closer to the smell of food. When we all arrived at the table, Monica had our plates full of food. By the twins' plates were the mandatory glasses of milk and orange juice. There was a full glass of apple juice on ice next to my plate.

"It's about time," she said standing as we took our seats at the table. "What took you all so long?'

"I guess I'm not use to dressing two energetic boys," I replied back. "It took me longer than I thought."

"Well, now you know what I go through every morning with them."

"Yes, I know now."

We all dug into our plates except the twins who barely touched their food. Apparently, all the excitement caused them to lose their appetite. After breakfast was over, I took the honor of making sure the twins brushed their teeth and finished packing a light back pack for our excursion. The back pack was filled with bottled water, hand sanitizer, and a few towels. Monica prepped the kitchen until it was crystal clean. Finally, I loaded up the Tahoe, secured the twins in their car seats, and we made our way to the zoo.

As expected, there was a traffic delay as we maneuvered south on I-85 closer to the Georgia Tech campus. Whether it was new construction, rain, or some fender bender you could always count on slow moving traffic even on the weekend. Suddenly, our vehicle came to a complete stop as I attempted to peek through the barrage of cars in front of us.

"Looks like we're going to be stuck here for a while," I said still looking forward. "You guys all right back there?"

"Yes," responded the twins simultaneously from the back of the Tahoe.

Their eyes and attention were placed fully on their favorite movie, *Happy Feet Two*, which was playing from the DVD console. Whoever came up with the bright idea of a mini monitor in a vehicle for viewing by back seat passengers must have had kids. It was a fool-proof system that kept them quiet and occupied. We could have been stuck in traffic for two minutes or two hours they wouldn't know the difference. As long as they had a movie to watch, the boys would be fine.

"I wonder what's going on now with this Atlanta traffic?" asked Monica turning her attention from a book she was reading to the view in front of us. "Do you think there's an accident, Aaron?"

"No, I didn't see any warnings on the visual traffic display board we passed a few minutes ago."

"All this backed-up traffic is giving me a headache. It's the weekend and I wasn't expecting this."

"So, I hope all the traffic we're going to have at our house for the twins' birthday is not going to give you a headache too."

"No way, I'll be all smiles regardless of how many people show up."

"So, who else did you invite besides the whole neighborhood?" I asked jokingly.

"Well, for starters, Shanna."

"Shanna," I shouted out. "She doesn't even have any kids."

"I know that, Aaron, but she would be a great help at the party anyway."

"Okay, who else?"

"I've invited a few teachers and administrators from the school. They all can't wait to come over with their kids."

"Come on, Monica, I know that's the tip of the iceberg. Who else is on the list?"

"There are also my parents and people they know with grandkids, a few of my girlfriends outside of work, and of course all our close neighbors."

"So, we are going to have a traffic jam at our house."

"Oh, Aaron, it's not going to be that bad. Besides, it's for the kids to enjoy themselves."

"Okay, sweetheart, it's your project and you're calling the shots."

"So, who are you inviting from your firm?" she asked.

"Just the normal crew to invite when we have an event involving kids," I replied back. "There is Jane with her grandkids, a few of my colleagues, and of course I couldn't omit Sebastian even though he doesn't have any kids either."

"Sebastian?"

"Yeah, Sebastian is coming, Monica."

"I hope you remember how he and Shanna almost killed each other by their looks alone at our wedding. We definitely don't want their lack of love for each other to disrupt our party."

"Don't worry I'll have a talk with him before then."

"What about inviting the new consultant at your firm over?"

"You mean, Tiffany."

"Yeah."

"No, I don't think so."

"Why not?"

"Because I don't think she's quite qualified to handle a house full of kids. And I never heard her talk about children so that may be out of her element."

"Okay, suit yourself. It was just a thought."

I never told Monica about my odd experience with Tiffany a few days ago in my office. In my opinion, some things were better left untold.

"Hey, look the traffic is finally moving again," I gladly said as we had something else to talk about.

"It's about time."

We were only a few minutes away once we passed downtown Atlanta and merged onto I-20 headed eastbound. Once I saw the Boulevard exit, I made a quick right and shortly we arrived at the zoo. As I pulled into the parking lot, the twins were still pre-occupied in the back seat. Finally, they noticed the vehicle had stopped again, but this time the engine was turned off.

Once inside the zoo, Brandon and Braylon were overly excited all together. The pair couldn't decide on where or what type of animals they wanted to see first. I held Brandon's hand while Monica held onto Braylon and we charted up the path to the zoo.

"Daddy, I want to see the zebras first," shouted out Brandon pulling on my hand.

"No, Brandon, let's see the elephants," said his brother trying to convince his sibling.

"I tell you what guys, let's make a compromise."

"What's a compromise, daddy?" asked Brandon.

"It's when we all agree on something. So let's say we all go see the giant panda named, Lun Lun, first."

"Okay," the both of them said in a not-so-energetic tone.

Lun Lun was the world-famous panda that came all the way from China. Rarely, do pandas survive in captivity but Lun Lun was the exception having lived in the Atlanta Zoo now for thirteen years. People from all over the world took pride in getting a glimpse of her day-to-day activities.

Throughout the day, we managed to see all the animals that peaked the curiosity of the twins. So when it was a quarter past seven, I decided we had enough fun for the day. The drive back to Sandy Springs was smooth as the twilight was almost upon us.

"I'm so glad we had fun today at the zoo," Monica said looking over at me.

"Yeah, I think the twins really enjoyed it," I said while noticing the twins were fast asleep from the rear-view mirror.

"So, what's in store for us tonight?"

"Once we get home, I'll put the twins in the bed. Then you and I can enjoy a glass of wine and call it a Netflix night."

"Aaron, that sounds good to me."

While I maintained the vehicle on the interstate, my wife surprised me. She smoothly eased over without distracting me and gave me a kiss.

"What was that for?" I asked looking at her for a brief second.

"Because I just wanted to give you a kiss," she explained. "And to tell you I love you."

"Monica, I love you too."

I refocused my attention back to the road and smiled. Steadily, I continued to drive anxious to make it to the confines of our home.

CHAPTER 7

The day had finally arrived which I had been waiting for. It was presentation Friday. Like all the previous mornings leading up to the big day this morning started off the same. Monica cooked a scrumptious breakfast, I kissed the twins good-bye, and oddly enough Mr. Newman was dressed in his normal attire walking Jewels.

When I arrived in my building's lobby, it was a normal morning as usual. Harold had a customer seated in one of the chairs giving him an excellent shine. Plus, there were two gentlemen, who were seated, waiting and another man standing up.

"Morning to you, Mr. Malone," Harold said in his normal friendly tone as he turned briefly from his customer.

"Good morning to you, Harold."

"I see those new shoes you're wearing with your suit are looking good."

"I owe it all to you."

A few days earlier I brought in a pair of shoes to Harold still new in the box. He touched up the shoes with a light coat of polish making them shine a bit. He constantly told me new shoes should always have a shine put on them before wearing. That way, they would last longer and look even better.

"You enjoy your day, sir. Oh, and by the way, good luck!"

"Thanks Harold."

When I reached the elevators, I paused and looked at my watch. It was precisely seven thirty and I was doing well on time. As many mornings before, a group boarded the elevator and it rushed upwards.

By the time I made it to my corner office, Jane was busy working at her desk. She looked up briefly as I approached her.

"Good morning, Mr. Malone," she said looking all bright-eyed for a Friday morning. "There's been a slight change with your presentation."

"Really," I said nervously as I stopped in front of her desk. "What has been changed?"

"The presentation has been moved up from eleven to ten. Additionally, Mr. Bradshaw would like for you to arrive at his office by nine-fifteen. His driver will take you, him, and his CFO to the site."

"Swell. Thanks Jane."

"Oh, Mr. Malone, thanks so much for inviting me and my grandchildren to your twins' birthday party next month. I just received the invitation from your wife in the mail yesterday."

"We look forward to having you and the grandkids there, Jane."

After my short dialogue with Jane, I walked into my office and closed the door behind me. I had a little more than two hours before the biggest presentation I'd ever made with Donaldson and Bradshaw was to occur. Gathering my thoughts and standing in the middle of my office, I began to recite my presentation as if a crowd was in front of me. I even unscrolled the designs and lay them on my workstation to make sure I wasn't leaving anything out.

When it was five minutes after nine, I grabbed the drafts and my briefcase and headed towards Mr. Bradshaw's office. Jane even gave me a final good luck farewell and bright smile. As I reached the entry to Mr. Bradshaw's office, his secretary gave me the approval to enter. Once inside, I saw Mr. Bradshaw was already joined by Mr. Black.

"Good morning, Aaron," said Mr. Bradshaw greeting me from behind his desk well dressed as usual. "I'm glad you made it a little early."

"Good morning to you, sir."

"Please come in and have a seat," he said pointing to the vacant chair in front of his desk. "I'm sure you're familiar with Mr. Black our firm's CFO."

"Yes, I am."

Mr. Black was already seated next to a chair that awaited me. He sat there well dressed also with a stoic look clutching his briefcase. I nodded to him in a friendly gesture and he did the same.

"Just to make sure everyone is aware," started out Mr. Bradshaw as the two of us looked on. "Ms. Towns' consulting firm, headquartered in New York City, will be in attendance this morning. Aaron, I'm sure you're familiar with them by now."

"Yes, Topaz Consulting Group is a well-established and reputable company."

"That they are, Aaron. That's why your presentation should go without any glitches. Besides them, there will be members from the press there too."

"Why will the press be there?" I asked looking anxious.

"I assume Topaz wants to garner as much attention to themselves on this project as possible. And who could blame them. This revitalization project is a great economy boost for the city of Atlanta."

"Well, I'm fully prepared for the presentation, sir."

"I'm confident you'll make a well-executed presentation. Those initial drafts I reviewed were tremendous."

"Thank you, sir."

"Alright, I believe our short briefing here is concluded," he said rising up from his chair and affixing his eyes on me. "Are there any further questions?"

"No, none at all," I replied.

"Very well, let's mount up and leave. My driver awaits us downstairs."

The three of us then made our way from Mr. Bradshaw's office and headed towards the main elevators. Before we did, Mr. Bradshaw stopped at his secretary desk momentarily.

"I'll be out of the office for an indefinite period of time today," he said in a bold voice. "You may advise my clients of the same."

"Yes sir, Mr. Bradshaw," she replied back.

After the exchange of words with the person who always knew his exact whereabouts, we continued on to the elevators. As we did, the entire office filled with workers scurried around looking busy. With the boss leading the way, I was ever-so-slightly behind him by his left elbow. To his right followed Mr. Black still clutching his briefcase. I even noticed Sebastian sneaking a peek at the rare scene. He smiled as to say 'good luck' and I returned a pleasant smile back at him.

Once we arrived at the bottom floor of the building, which housed Mr. Bradshaw's fleet of vehicles, his personal driver named Charles greeted us. Charles had been loyal to the firm for many years and was closer to Mr. Bradshaw's age. He was dressed in a suit and positioned himself outside a black GMC Yukon Denali next to the elevators.

"Good morning, sir," Charles said opening the rear passenger door for Mr. Bradshaw.

"Good morning, Charles. As you can see Mr. Black and Mr. Malone will be joining us for our short trip."

"Yes, I see, sir."

Mr. Bradshaw made his way into the vehicle first, followed by Mr. Black, then myself. The inside of the Denali was custom designed with the rear interior seats facing one another. This made it easier for the occupants to discuss any business at hand. Mr. Black took the seat opposite but facing Mr. Bradshaw. I sat directly next to Mr. Bradshaw. Once we all were inside, Charles closed the door and took his position in the driver's seat.

"Charles, as you know, our destination is the old General Motors assembly plant in Doraville," ordered Mr. Bradshaw from the rear seat. "We need to arrive before ten o'clock."

"Yes, sir, Mr. Bradshaw," said Charles putting the vehicle in gear and exiting the parking garage. "I'll have you there shortly."

As expected, Charles maneuvered the crystal clean Denali through the hectic traffic on I-285. To no one's surprise there was still a steady flow of the early-morning rush-hour traffic that plagued the interstate. Charles, being an experienced driver, delicately wheeled the two-ton vehicle in and out of traffic. We still had ten minutes to spare once we reached the entrance to the old assembly plant.

"We have arrived at the old General Motors assembly plant, sir," said Charles from the driver's seat as the vehicle moved slowly.

"We have indeed, Charles," replied Mr. Bradshaw looking through his passenger side tinted window. "You never seem to amaze me. Always prompt, effective, and efficient as usual."

"Thank you, sir. I'll pull over to the area where all the other cars have gathered for your convenience."

"That will be fine."

Since Topaz Consulting Group was the liaison for the revitalization project, they had the presentation area all decked out. The meeting area was just outside the former main entrance doors to the assembly plant. There you could see the location had a green felt-like material that covered the ground over a flat seven-hundred square foot area. Positioned on top of the green material were chairs for the participants. Directly in front of the chairs, were a rectangular table, billboard, and podium. From here, one had a panoramic view of the old industrial site, which was perfect for explaining my presentation.

After the vehicle was parked, Charles got out and opened our doors so we could exit. With Mr. Bradshaw in front, we joined the individuals who were already positioned in the meeting area a few feet away. Tiffany was the first person who greeted us upon our arrival.

"Good morning, Mr. Bradshaw," said Tiffany extending her right hand to him.

"Good morning, Tiffany," he said shaking her hand.

"We at Topaz Consulting Group are overly excited this day has arrived."

"We are also, Tiffany. You already met Mr. Black, my CFO of the firm and of course Aaron whom you've worked closely with so far."

"Yes, indeed, Mr. Bradshaw."

Mr. Black, who was still clutching his briefcase as if it was filled with gold bullions simply nodded and gave a firm handshake to Tiffany. I in turned shook her hand, smiled, and said hello.

"Well, let me introduce you all to the rest of the participants here this morning," she said while the eager on-lookers waited behind her.

For the next few minutes, Tiffany introduced us to two gentlemen with her firm, the designated project manager, two site engineers, a few dignitaries, and members who represented the architect press. After that, Mr. Bradshaw took control and made his presence felt at the podium.

"Good morning, attendees," he said speaking loudly into the microphone while everyone took their seats. "I am Thomas Bradshaw, owner of Donaldson and Bradshaw, and the firm which spearheads the General Motors revitalization project."

Mr. Bradshaw gave a quick overview of his firm as the intimate crowd listened patiently. Even members of the press took a few photos of him as the flash from their high-resolution cameras sounded off. Then he finally got to the main part of introducing me.

"And now without further a due," he continued in his speech. "The man you've been waiting on and responsible for this great project, Mr. Aaron Malone.

As I took the podium, the crowd gave me a warm reception but my nerves were on edge a bit. Of course, the flashes continued before I started my speech. With the initial drafts posted neatly on the billboard behind me, I covered all the basics for the project. Once my speech was concluded, I received a barrage of questions from the audience.

"How did you compensate for the retail spaces versus the land primarily used for homes and high-rise condos?" asked the first engineer from the crowd.

"Yeah, and what about how you forecasted for the flow of traffic from the nearby Marta station," followed the second engineer. "Will it help or hinder with the development?"

I answered both of their questions impressively as I even caught Tiffany smiling. Mr. Bradshaw seemed as if he was glowing like he was a proud parent and I was his son. He knew it wasn't a mistake he assigned me as the senior designer for the task. As more questions came in, I answered them swiftly and more convincingly than the last. When the questions had ended, I suggested we walk through a portion of the site so the crowd could get a better visual of my designs. They loved it, shaking their heads in approval while looking at each other.

By the time it was all over, two hours had elapsed when Mr. Bradshaw took the podium for the second time. He began his thank you and farewell speech to the audience which continued to listen eagerly.

"As a token of my appreciation," he said. "I would like to invite everyone to join me for a mixer at the Twelve Hotel this evening at six o'clock. Mr. Aaron Malone was actually a main contributing designer for the hotel. There you'll be able to see firsthand one of his many achievements while listening to live jazz and enjoying dinner with cocktails."

"Is that hotel near the Four Seasons where we are staying?" asked one of the dignitaries in the crowd.

"It's not too far," replied Mr. Bradshaw. "But don't worry, I'll send a car to pick up your party and anyone else who may need transportation."

After Mr. Bradshaw finished the specifics about the mixer slated for later that evening, everyone continued to mingle for a while. Tiffany took this opportunity to congratulate me personally on my speech.

"Very impressive, Aaron," she said as we moved away from the crowd. "I think your presentation solidified your firm's mark with everyone in attendance today."

"Why thank you, Tiffany," I modestly stated. "But I think it was okay. I still have a long way to go before the final drafts are completed."

"Come on, Aaron, don't worry about that. Tonight is all about celebrating and having a little fun. You do remember what I said about all work and no play, right?"

"Yes, Tiffany, I remembered."

"I'll see you this evening at the Twelve Hotel."

"I'm sure I will."

When our short conversation ended, Tiffany joined the members of her consulting firm. I fitted in with Mr. Bradshaw who was having a discussion with the press. Mr.

Black was there too standing next to him. Afterwards, the three of us found ourselves in the back of the Denali while Charles navigated us through the traffic. The day was a success so far but the thrill of the evening was yet to come.

CHAPTER 8

It was three forty-five in the afternoon as I sat reclined back in my office chair behind my desk. I glanced out my office window to notice the traffic on I-285 starting to bottleneck on a Friday afternoon. In the mist of paying attention to the traffic, my office phone rang and I promptly answered it.

"Hi, honey," said my wife on the other end in a cheerful mood.

"Hello Monica," I replied back still watching the traffic. "So how was your day?"

"Aaron, it was just another routine day at North Atlanta High School. But that's not what I'm calling you about. How did your presentation go this morning?"

"It went very well. Mr. Bradshaw was pleased and the group of individuals I presented the initial designs to were impressed."

"I am so proud of you! I knew you would be an impact at your presentation today."

"Thank you, sweetheart. But I owe a lot to you for giving me pointers while adamantly listening to my practice speech over and over again."

"That's what a good wife is supposed to do."

"Hey, we should celebrate later tonight. I have to attend a mixer Mr. Bradshaw surprised everyone with that starts at six. I should only be there for a few hours."

"Aaron, did you forget?"

"Forget about what?"

"Tonight, the twins and I are sleeping over my parent's house."

"That's right, Monica, I totally forgot. You scheduled the date a few weeks ago."

"We can always celebrate in a few days or later. You should enjoy yourself tonight with your colleagues and friends anyway."

"Yeah, maybe your right."

"Yes, I am. You deserve to enjoy the success you're having with the firm."

"So, where are you now?"

"I'm driving over to the house to pack a few items for tonight. Then I'll make my way over to my parent's house before traffic really picks up."

"Thank God we live in-town. You should see the view of traffic from my office."

"It seems like the decision to buy the house in Sandy Springs, instead of Conyers, is paying off."

"From the looks up here, I would say yes."

"Well, I'll talk to you later, honey. Enjoy your night and I love you."

"I love you too, Monica. Be sure to kiss the boys goodnight for me."

As soon as my conversation ended with Monica, in strolls my buddy from Florida State University. I thought he would have arrived sooner but apparently he was preoccupied.

"Well, well, well, if it isn't Mr. Successful in the flesh," Sebastian said taking a seat in front of my desk.

"So, where did you hear that from?" I asked turning my reclined swivel chair towards him.

"Aaron, it's all over the office today that you did a fantastic job on your presentation."

"Thanks, Sebastian, but it really was not that big of a deal."

"Either way congratulations are in order because you deserve it. It looks like Mr. Bradshaw may be positioning you for a VP spot in the near future."

"I think you may be going overboard on that one but I appreciate you being so optimistic. So, you probably heard about the mixer this evening?"

"Indeed I did," he said smiling and leaning back in his chair. "So, you'll be celebrating tonight with the bigwigs, huh?"

"I wouldn't say they were all that," I said. "They are just a few influential people who were at the presentation this morning. And speaking about celebrating, we're having the twins' birthday party at our house next month and you're officially invited."

"Are my favorite twins having another birthday already again?"

"Yes, Sebastian, they're turning four. Monica even promised to invite a few of her single girlfriends just for you."

"Well, I can't refuse an invitation like that. So, how are your other celebration plans coming along?"

"You mean my fifth-year wedding anniversary?"

"Yeah, don't tell me you forgot to plan something."

"No, I actually have Jane working on it. She's great at planning stuff like that since I've been super busy with my designs and presentation."

"That's good because you're going to need a big celebration, especially if you've conquered the five-year itch."

"Come on, Sebastian, don't start with the whole five-year itch theory," I said laughing while waving my left hand in his face showing off my diamond wedding band.

"Some women are attracted to married men more."

Just then his cell phone rings and interrupts our dialog about marriage. He glances at his phone, smiles, and then sends the call to his voice mail.

"So, who was that?" I asked being nosey.

"Oh, it's just one of my friends checking in on me. She's probably calling only to confirm our date for tonight."

"Big plans for the weekend, I assume?"

"Not really. Just the routine dinner and a movie date," he said standing up and placing the cell phone in his front pocket of his slacks. "I just came by to once again say congratulations and hope you enjoy yourself this evening."

"Thanks for all the support," I replied back. "I'll see you on Monday morning."

"See you then," he said finally exiting my office.

I spent the next hour or so returning a few phone calls and emails. Then briefly started thinking about the early design specs for phases two and three. Even though it was a victorious day, it was only a matter of time before Mr. Bradshaw would be seeking the next installments of designs. When five o'clock rolled around, I grabbed my jacket and decided to make the voyage to Atlantic Station. I figured I would be moving at a snail's pace during the next hour due to the Friday evening traffic in Atlanta.

When I arrived at the Twelve Hotel, it was fifteen minutes past six o'clock. I pulled right up to the hotel's entrance and allowed the valet to park my car. Then I walked through the electronic sensored doors and entered the lobby. There in the short distance ahead of me was Mr. Bradshaw and a few dignitaries from the presentation. Standing next to them, were two men from Topaz Consulting Group. They all were at the bar enjoying a drink. I casually walked over to get reacquainted.

"Good evening, everyone," I calmly said as the gentlemen at the bar had their backs slightly towards me.

Mr. Bradshaw was the first to turn around I guessed because he noticed my voice. Then everyone else followed.

"Aaron, you're here," said Mr. Bradshaw with a royal smile and holding a martini glass in his left hand.

"Sorry, I'm a few minutes late, sir. You know how this Atlanta traffic can be on Fridays."

"No problem at all, Aaron. We were all just actually getting started on our first drink. So what will you have?"

I thought for a few seconds but it seemed like time was moving in slow motion. It was as if Mr. Bradshaw was asking me the million-dollar question and I wanted to make sure I had the right answer. I looked at the clear solution that filled his martini glass and the green olive that perfectly accentuated it.

"I'll have a vodka martini," I said giving my answer.

"Excellent choice," exclaimed Mr. Bradshaw holding up his cocktail. "That's what I'm drinking. Bartender, please give this man a vodka martini and another round for whatever everyone else is drinking."

"Right away, sir," swiftly responded the busy bartender quickly grabbing a few glasses.

"Well, Mr. Malone, we had a chance to view the Twelve Hotel before you arrived," said one of the gentlemen from Topaz Consulting Group. "We are very impressed."

"Why thank you but please call me, Aaron. So what in particular did you like about the hotel?"

"How seamless and clean the interior designs are," answered the second gentlemen with Topaz. "It's modern, contemporary, sleek and stylish."

"I concur," interjected one of the dignitaries standing next to Mr. Bradshaw. "It's a job well done."

"Why thank you, gentlemen," I replied. "I'm so honored and pleased you all approve of the hotel."

By now, the busy bartender had completed everyone's drink and I found my hand clutching onto a martini glass. The rest of the men had secured their drinks also.

"Yes, Aaron is quite an asset to our firm," said Mr. Bradshaw as everyone took a sip from their cocktails. "He has made us all, including me, very proud we have him on our team."

"Yes, I do believe Aaron is quite the asset," said a noticeable feminine voice from behind me.

As I turned around, it was Tiffany who was fashionably late but well worth it. She finally made it downstairs from her temporary condo residence at the hotel. I fixed my eyes on her all black party dress which symbolized power and flair. It wasn't anything conservative like the wardrobe I was use to seeing her in. This dress showed her tight curves, sexy legs, and even her breasts seemed bigger.

Glancing down, she kept the black theme going with designer black heels showing off her red-colored well pedicure toes.

"Ms. Towns, don't you look stunning," said Mr. Bradshaw as the rest of the gentlemen perked up at the bar. "We are so glad you could join us."

"I wouldn't have missed this opportunity for anything," she replied back. "Besides, it's the weekend and I think we all need to let our hair down a bit."

"With that being said, may I offer you a drink?" asked Mr. Bradshaw still intrigued by her appearance.

"Of course," she said without any hesitation. "I'll have a cosmopolitan."

As before, Mr. Bradshaw beckoned the bartender who quickly fixed Tiffany's drink. For a short period, we all made small talk at the bar until a female hostess approached us. She told Mr. Bradshaw the table he had reserved for dinner was now ready and she promptly led us there.

"So Aaron, I just wanted to once again congratulate you for your excellent presentation today," said Tiffany as I held her chair out for her while she took a seat at the table.

"Well, I am just glad that part is finally over," I said taking my seat next to her.

"Just remember to take account of your accomplishments along the way. It will make your road to continued success much smoother."

"No one ever explained it to me like that but I do agree with what you are saying."

We both lifted up our glasses and toasted to her point. Then simultaneously, we drank while she looked into my eyes. The ambiance at the hotel was magnificent that evening as the live jazz band was playing a classic Miles Davis tune. Mr. Bradshaw's party had the best seat in the house for dinner, drinks, and simply listening to good music.

CHAPTER 9

By the time I glanced down at my watch, I noticed it was a quarter past ten o'clock. Tiffany must have noticed the same by her comment.

"Is it time to return to the wife and kids?" she asked without any reservations.

"Yeah, just about," I said finishing off my drink. "In my world, anytime after ten is considered late."

"Well, let me walk you to the lobby's front door."

"Tiffany, you don't have to go through any trouble to do that."

"Aaron, I don't mind. Besides, I could use a little fresh air as it's a bit stuffy in here. Just let me run to the little girls' room first."

"Okay, if you insist. I'll wait right here for you."

I quickly stood up from my seat and assisted her by pulling her chair away from the table. She rose and proceeded towards exiting our area. When she did, apparently the top of her left heel caught the back end of my chair's leg. Tiffany's body lunged forward and her lower torso flipped halfway around while she was in mid-air. Permanently, she landed right smack on her derriere. The incident took all but a split millisecond to occur.

"Oh my God!" yelled a slightly intoxicated woman sitting next to our table. "She fell."

"Tiffany, are you alright?" I asked as I rushed over to her body and kneeled down.

"Yes, Aaron, I'm fine. The only thing that is hurting is my pride right now."

Mr. Bradshaw quickly noticed what had happened and rushed to his feet. Then he made his way over to us. The rest of the members at the table looked on in amazement while the gentlemen from Topaz stood up.

"Ms. Towns are you okay?" asked Mr. Bradshaw stooping over us.

"Mr. Bradshaw I'm fine," she said looking embarrassed having caused a scene. "I must have had one too many cosmopolitans which made me light-headed. Either that or the clumsy side of me is starting to show."

By now, the hotel's service manager who was in the vicinity and witnessed the occurrence had arrived at our table. He stood by Mr. Bradshaw bending down.

" Ma'am, are you okay?" asked the service manager in a sincere voice.

"Yes, everyone, I am fine," reiterated Tiffany to the small crowd standing over her.

"Ma'am, as a precaution we will need to file an accident report per the hotel's guidelines."

"Please just send someone to my room in the morning regarding the report," said Tiffany. "I live upstairs in the condo residence and right now I just want to go lay down."

"What's your name, ma'am?" asked the service manager pulling a small pocket notebook and pen from his suit's interior pocket.

"It's Tiffany Towns."

"Aaron, why don't you see to it that Ms. Towns makes it to her room upstairs," announced Mr. Bradshaw taking control of the situation.

"Sure, Mr. Bradshaw, that's no problem. I was just on my way out but I can assist her before I go."

"Very well, Aaron," he said. "I'll see you first thing Monday morning. And you get some rest yourself, Ms. Towns."

"I will," she said still showing signs of embarrassment.

I bent down and retrieved Tiffany's small purse from the floor and handed it to her. Then I slowly helped her to her feet where our arms interlocked. I could tell she was still woozy and carefully led her to the hotel's elevators.

"So what floor do you live on?"

"I'm on the twenty-fifth floor."

Once inside the elevator I pressed the designated number as we were on our way. When we arrived at her residence, she gave me the key which was similar to a credit card. I fumbled it momentarily and then we entered. Her place was completely dark. The inside was only illuminated from the outside city lights cascading in from the large living-room windows.

"You probably need to take two aspirins just to be on the safe side," I told her as we stood in the dark kitchen with the closed front door behind us. "Do you have any?"

"Yes, the aspirins are across the hall on the bathroom counter."

Knowing exactly where the bathroom was from my designs, I raced over for the bottle of aspirins. When I returned to the dark kitchen, Tiffany was still waiting in her same spot. I popped the container open and poured two aspirin pills into my right palm. She then lunged both of her hands towards me. Most women think all men are dogs. I guess this was the point where the bulldog in me came out. I grabbed the back of Tiffany's hair with my left hand and slightly bent her head back.

"Oh, Aaron, I love the pain," she yelled out.

I teased her by kissing her full and thick bottom lip only. To give her the pain she so enjoyed I bit the same lip while keeping a firm grip on her hair.

"Ouch dammit!" she yelled again in pain. "That shit is turning me on!"

Our tongues finally met and we found ourselves kissing in the dark kitchen. The two aspirins fell from my right palm onto the floor and I used the same hand to fondle her luscious breasts with nipples fully hardened. As I released the grip of her hair and raised her onto the granite countertop a stream of light reflected off my diamond wedding ring. I went to remove the band from my finger before the devilish act was about to occur.

"No, leave it on."

"What?"

"I said leave it on."

"Why?"

"Because the sight of a married man who is about to fuck me really turns me on!"

She spread her legs wide open while keeping her back erect on the kitchen countertop. Her back wasn't the only thing that was erect by now. I smoothly moved her dress from her thighs up to her Coke bottle shaped waist. By now, her breasts were out of her dress and I filled them into my welcoming mouth. As I rotated sucking her nipples I used one of my hands and eased it between her legs. That's when I found out she had no panties on so I quickly rubbed on her clit.

"Damn, you're wetter than ever," I said in a heated tone with my dick bulging through my slacks. "I'm ready to enter you."

"Not until I please you first," she stated hopping off the counter.

She kept her eyes fixed onto mine and kneeled down while her hands found my belt buckle. My pants with my boxers in them fell to my ankles. Then she gave me satisfying head.

"Tiffany, that feels so good!"

She made the tip of my hard dick reach the back of her throat. Then like some magic act she was able to use her tongue to reach and lick my balls. It was the ultimate pleasure.

"How does it feel to have someone other than your wife sucking your dick?" she asked while taking me out of her mouth for only a moment.

"It feels good! Now get back on the counter."

"Not yet, Aaron. It turns me on that you're being turned on."

She quickly placed me back into her mouth before saying another word. I was at her disposal but enjoying the view and pleasure at the same time.

"Okay, that's enough!" I shouted out in frantic tone and pried her off my dick. Immediately, I raised her back on the top of the kitchen countertop where she gladly opened her legs. Then, I took the head of my rock hard dick and massaged her pussy lips up and down without entering her. "Wait, I need something."

"They're in my purse."

I frantically grabbed her small purse which she conveniently laid on the countertop when we first entered her place. Once opened, I found three Trojan Magnum extra large lubricated condoms individually wrapped. I picked one and tore the wrapper off the condom.

"Hurry, Aaron, I'm so hot and horny."

"Here it comes," I said as I carefully unrolled the condom onto my erect dick. Then I finally entered her.

"Oh yes," she screamed out as I pressed forward into her.

"Is that what you always wanted?" I asked as I slowly withdrew my dick and began to enter her again but this time much deeper.

"Awww," she screamed in pleasure while clawing her nails into my back.

Then in a hurry, I picked her off the counter by her waist as she held onto me by my neck. Her legs dangled from my forearms while I kept my dick firmly inside her. We stumbled two steps backwards towards the front door. Once there, I pushed her back up against it. I grabbed the door handle with my right hand and placed my left hand on the opposite side where it connected to a door hinge. It was in this position I stroked her harder than ever and both of our pelvises met.

"That's what I want!"

"Are you sure, Tiffany?"

"Hell yeah, fuck me you married mother fucker!"

For the next fifteen minutes, I kept her in that position stroking and pounding every inch of me into what seemed to be an endless pit. My adrenaline was racing throughout my body and I was sweating profusely. I kept her in the same position and moved backwards from the door. Her legs still dangling from my forearms, I found the sofa next to the large windows in the living room. I sat back while she rode me and she finally came.

"Come on and follow me," she said rising off my erected dick, standing up, and not wanting to take a break.

I obeyed her directions and stood up taking off my heavily sweat soaked shirt. Then, I removed my pants and boxers which were still around my ankles. After that, I ripped the remaining dress off of her.

She grabbed my hand and led me onto the balcony. The April night air was balmy and cool but our hot bodies didn't care. Next to Tiffany's gorgeous body the view of downtown Atlanta was spectacular.

"Now, fuck me in my ass like I love it," she ordered while carefully bending over the balcony railing.

Within seconds my dick had penetrated the walls of her anal cavity and was flowing freely into her. As our bodies clapped together, I grabbed the back of her long hair and pulled her head up. She would have no choice but to observe the city landscape while I was in her.

"Now give it to me more," I said in a controlling voice.

"Hell yeah, Aaron, fuck me like that!" she screamed at the top of her lungs.

Her arrogance and screams turned me on even more. I penetrated deeper.

"Is that deep enough for you?"

"Deeper dammit!"

"So you really want me to fuck you harder, huh?"

"Uh huh," she cried out in her sexy voice.

"Okay, take your right leg and extend it onto the railing."

She complied and it was at this position where our sexual performance peaked out. In and out I entered her while bending over stimulating her clit with my hand. I stroked harder and harder until I was almost there.

"I'm about to come," I growled out

"Yes, Aaron, I'm almost there too."

"Here it is!"

"Oh, your throbbing dick feels so good inside me. I'm coming with you."

When our sexual escapade was over, she led me back inside but this time to her bedroom. We quietly immersed ourselves under the covers. Regrettably, I had done something I thought would never happen in a million years. I failed to remain faithful to my wife. To make matters worse, I validated Sebastian's five-year itch theory.

CHAPTER 10

Monday morning had arrived and it was back to the grind at Donaldson and Bradshaw as usual. Only this time, I had to deal with the thoughts of my transgressions with Tiffany which occurred on Friday night. As I took my morning stroll past Jane's desk, I spoke before she had an opportunity to.

"Good morning, Jane," I said while standing in front of her desk.

"Good morning to you, Mr. Malone," she replied cordially. "How was your weekend?"

"It was good. And yours?"

"It was delightful as usual, Mr. Malone."

"Well, that's great, Jane. Any messages for me this morning?"

"No, not one."

"That's odd, especially for a Monday morning. Well, I'm off to my office to get some work done."

"Oh, Mr. Malone, there was an early delivery for you this morning."

"There was a delivery for me?"

"Yes, a courier service arrived with fresh flowers addressed to you. They had special instructions to only place them on your desk. Of course, I signed for the delivery."

"Who would send me flowers?"

"They were actually a dozen red roses in a vase with a note attached. I assumed they were from your wife."

"My wife?" I stated with a perplexed look.

"Yes, Mr. Malone. Maybe since you are always sending her red roses she thought to return the favor back to you."

"Yeah, maybe you're right, Jane," I said but thinking to myself Monica had never sent me flowers in all our years of being married.

I walked into my office and closed the door behind me. Just as Jane had described the vase containing the twelve roses were positioned in the middle of my desk. But these weren't ordinary roses they were culturally grown. My curiosity was killing me, so I finally grabbed the note that was attached. The note read: *I'm glad you decided to come out and play.* I knew instantly the roses were from Tiffany. I shredded the note then stared at the roses trying to decide what to do next.

"Mr. Malone are you available?" asked Jane through my phone's intercom system breaking my concentration.

"Yes Jane, I'm here," I said in an angry tone. "What is it?"

"Sir, it's Ms. Tiffany Towns on line four for you?

"Who?" I asked stalling Jane trying to gather my thoughts as I took a seat in my chair.

"Ms. Towns, the consultant, who was here in the office not too long ago."

"Oh, yeah Jane, I remember her now. You can just transfer her through."

As my number four line constantly blinked I simply waited before answering. I took a deep breath and picked up the phone's handset pressing the corresponding line.

"This is Aaron," I answered in a calm voice.

"Well good morning, Aaron, I see you finally made it to your desk," said Tiffany sounding sultry on the other end. "Do you like your roses?"

"They're nice."

"Listen, I'm working at my firm's satellite office today downtown on Marietta Street. I've picked up a new assignment but figured we could do lunch today."

"Lunch?"

"I figured Maggiano's or Morton's if you prefer. They're both in Buckhead on Peachtree Road."

"Yeah, I know where they both are located."

"Or maybe we can just rendezvous at a more intimate place like my condo for a quickie."

"Tiffany, slow down because we need to talk."

"Talk about what, Aaron?"

"About what happened on Friday night?"

"You mean how you literally fucked the shit out of me?"

"It was a mistake," I said in a firm tone and taking a stance on which way the conversation was going. "It shouldn't have happened and it won't again."

"What do you mean a mistake!" she shouted out in a defensive tone. "Was it a mistake the way you purposely allowed me to suck your dick? Or how about how you continuously fucked me until I came? Was that a mistake too, Aaron?"

"I have a wife and two kids and I'm not going to lose it to a one-night-stand. Besides, Tiffany, we both probably had a little too much to drink."

"So now you're blaming it on the alcohol."

"No, I'm saying it was just poor judgment on both of us."

"Aaron, I'm not trying to make you upset so please don't be mad at me. I realize you have a wife and kids but keep in mind I like married men."

The more we spoke the more our ideas and views spread further apart. I wanted out and she continued to push in.

"Tiffany, there's nothing further to discuss here," I said firmly trying to get her off my phone. "We both should remain professional about the situation. From my understanding, our firm only retained your services for the initial designs on the revitalization project. As you know, those designs were completed last week."

"So that's how you want it, huh?"

"That's the way it has to be."

"Well, I guess you're calling the shots right now, Mr. Malone. But I'll definitely see you later."

Before I could respond to her facetious comment, she quickly hung up. I, in turn, slammed the receiver down in a sign of disbelief of what had just happened. After interlocking my fingers together and placing them on my chest, I leaned back in my chair. Exhaling, I then swiveled the chair towards the window and back to my desk again. When I did, I noticed the dozen red roses right in my face as if they were smiling at me. In an angry haste, I grabbed the bottom of the vase and flung it as hard as I could to the wall in front of me across the room. The vase shattered into many pieces while the water was soaked up by the thick carpet on the floor. Scattered all over the floor were the twelve red roses.

"Oh my God, Mr. Malone, are you alright?" shouted Jane barging into my office without knocking. "What happened in here?"

"The roses slipped out of my hand when I tried to move them," I said quickly standing up and remained behind my desk.

"But how did they slip out of your hand when the debris is near your door and you're behind the desk?"

"Jane, we just need to call housekeeping right away and have them clean up this mess."

"Okay, Mr. Malone," she said hesitantly and looking at me in a strange manner. "But I'm going to personally pick up these roses because they are too pretty to be on the floor."

For the next few seconds, Jane carefully picked up each rose and placed them delicately into her arms. I stood there looking foolish thinking how did I let my emotions get the best of me.

"Mr. Malone, I'm going to find another vase, fill it with water, and bring these lovely roses back to you," she said after gathering all the roses off the floor. "Besides, we wouldn't want your wife coming by and not seeing the roses she sent you."

"I guess you're right, Jane."

"I'll be right back, shortly."

"Jane, do me a favor."

"Yes, Mr. Malone."

"When you find the vase for the roses, just place them on your desk."

"But why?" she asked with a puzzled look on her face.

"Well, my desk is cluttered enough and I wouldn't want another accident ruining my new designs I'm working on."

"Whatever you wish, Mr. Malone."

"Jane, one more thing before you go."

"Yes."

"Call Sebastian Carter right away and transfer him to my main extension."

"Yes, sir."

Jane exited my office and I sat back down still disgusted. Housekeeping arrived expeditiously cleaning up the mess I had made in a jiffy. Then right on cue, Jane patched Sebastian over to my main line.

"Hello, Sebastian."

"Morning, Aaron. I just received a call from your secretary stating you needed to speak with me. Did you need help with the new designs?"

"No, I think I have the designs covered but we need to talk."

"About what?" he asked as if my comment peaked his interest like never before.

"Man talk," I quickly said.

"Okay, Aaron. How about we meet in the firm's athletic club downstairs during the lunch hour? We can work out and talk at the same time."

"Yeah, that's a good idea. I always keep a fresh change of workout gear in my locker downstairs."

"So is one o'clock good with you?"

"That's perfect, Sebastian. I'll see you then."

When one o'clock arrived I told Jane where I would be for the next hour or so and made my way downstairs. The firm's athletic club was only a few floors down. Mr. Bradshaw found it to be a convenient way for his workers to stay in shape without any excuses. All employees enjoyed free membership and could work out before their shift, during lunch, or after hours.

In the men's dressing room, I changed my attire and headed out to the aerobic area of the club. Within this area, there were rows upon rows of treadmills with mini monitors attached. People were walking or running to various speeds like robots. I quickly found Sebastian on one making small talk with a female on one side of his treadmill. Then I approached him.

"I thought I'd find you in here working out on the treadmills," I said walking up to him on the opposite side of the woman.

"Glad to see you made it, Aaron," he replied turning away from the woman. "Just step up on the treadmill next to mine. I'm five minutes into my thirty-five minute walk and sprint."

The woman next to him plugged in her earphones and turned her attention to the monitor keeping a brisk pace. Now, I had joined Sebastian in the steady flow of robots.

"So what's so important that you had to talk to me about?" he asked maintaining his speed.

"Something happened to me this weekend that I don't feel right about," I said turning on my treadmill to a medium pace.

"Did it involve the wife and kids?"

"Not directly."

"So what is it?"

"It was at the mixer last Friday night."

Sebastian turned his head towards me slowly and looked me squarely in my eyes. He glared at me for a few seconds before he spoke again.

"No, Aaron, don't tell me what I'm thinking is right. And it happened with the consultant?"

"We had been drinking all night, Sebastian. Then unexpectedly before I leave she falls at the dining table and there's a commotion."

"What?" he said almost falling off his treadmill. "So what happened next?"

"So Mr. Bradshaw and the service manager rushed over to make sure she was alright."

"Yeah, go on."

"And of all people, Mr. Bradshaw suggested I walk her upstairs to her condo to make sure she would be alright."

There was brief pause and then Sebastian figured it out. He made a large grin that covered his entire face.

"Aaron, you are an old sly dog. I didn't know you had it in you."

"I swear, Sebastian, it wasn't planned. To make matters worse, she sent me a dozen red roses this morning."

"So I don't get it, Aaron. What's the problem?"

"She called me this morning and I told her what happened on Friday night was a big mistake. She strictly got upset about my rejection towards her."

"Well, do you blame her for that?"

"What do you mean, Sebastian?"

"Look, Aaron, I know you're a smart guy but you can't screw a woman's brain out on Friday night and call it quits on Monday morning. It just doesn't work. Their delicate and emotional creatures and, most importantly, they hold grudges."

"I'm a married man and want to keep it that way. I have no intention of getting into deeper waters with her even if she is okay with it."

"Simply sweep it under the rug and forget about it."

"Yeah, that's what I plan on doing."

CHAPTER 11

"Daddy, where are you going?" asked Brandon running up to me while I had one hand on the knob of the front door."

"Daddy has to go to work today, Brandon."

"But it's Saturday. You're supposed to watch cartoons with us today."

"Daddy has to get a lot of work done today," I said looking down into his disappointed eyes. "But I promise to watch cartoons with you next time."

"Okay I love you, daddy."

"I love you too, son," I said as I bent down and hugged my son. "Now run along to the living room and join your brother watching TV."

He scampered off before I could get the request out of my mouth good. As I intended to make my departure this time, my wife approached me.

"Here you are honey," she said handling me a brown paper bag.

"What is this?" I asked taking possession of the bag.

"It's your favorite. Deli sliced turkey, ham, and salami on a wheat roll. Plus, I added all the extra trimmings you like also."

Sound tasty, sweetheart. Thanks for the lunch."

"I figured you would get sort of hungry working in the office this Saturday."

"Yeah, you figured right."

"How long do you plan on working today?" she asked.

"I figure maybe until mid-afternoon. I really have to get the next phases of these designs to Mr. Bradshaw by next week."

"Well, the twins and I will be fine. I'm taking them to my parent's house later. They can enjoy themselves over there while Shanna and I go to the hair salon today."

"Oh, that's right, it's your weekend to visit the salon again."

"Yes, I want to look and feel great for the twins' birthday party next Saturday. And Shanna is taking me to a new salon in Buckhead she recently visited."

"You already look great to me, sweetheart," I said before giving her a kiss. "I'll see you later on."

"I'll see you soon, Aaron."

I opened the front door and soaked in the bright sunny rays. It seemed as if it was going to be another gorgeous spring day in Atlanta but I would be stuck in a stuffy office. Despite that, I knew my work was priority and it paid the bills. So I hopped in my Audi as I had done so many times before and headed to work.

By noon, Monica had managed to get the twins dressed, loaded the SUV with a few of their favorite toys, and was now pulling into her parent's driveway. Dr. Carmichael would be extremely excited to see his grandchildren. Over the last month or so, he was busy lecturing, promoting one of his prior books, and still had time to teach at Emory. With all that going on, he barely had time to see the twins.

Before Monica had a chance to turn the ignition off, out rushes her mother from the house. She was always elated about seeing her grandchildren no matter what.

"Monica, where are my favorite grandchildren today?" she asked walking up to the driver's side door.

"Well hello to you too, mom," Monica responded as she turned off the SUV's engine and exited the vehicle. "They're in the back seat taking a nap."

The twins had only been asleep briefly during the short drive from Monica's home to her parent's house. It wasn't usual for them to fall asleep when riding in the back seat.

"Well, I'm going to have to wake them up because I just can't help it." She calmly opens the rear passenger door and finds both boys in their car seats with their eyes closed. "Brandon and Braylon wake up, its grandma."

As if her sweet voice casted a magical spell over the two, they immediately awoke from their trance. They rubbed their eyes with their little hands and realized where they were.

"Grandma!" yelled the twins out loud and extended their arms.

"Hello, you two precious boys. Now, let's get both of you out of these car seats and into the house."

Meanwhile, Monica had made her way around to the rear of the vehicle. There she retrieved a bag with miscellaneous items including toys. After she closed the vehicle's truck, she noticed her mother and the twins were walking towards the front door hand-in-hand. She secured the bag and quickly caught up with them.

By the time everyone reached the front door, Dr. Carmichael was standing in the doorway. He was dressed casually and still had the television remote control in one hand.

"There's my grandpa!" shouted Brandon as he pulled away from his grandmother to greet him.

"Grandpa!" Braylon shouted also after his brother.

Dr. Carmichael bent down and hugged his two grandchildren after they rushed towards him. He was still smiling after he hugged them.

"We've been expecting you all," he said in his distinguished voice still standing in the doorway. "Come on inside."

When everyone finally made it inside to the foyer of the home, there was an exchange of hugs between Monica and her parents. Then Monica placed the twins' bag down by the front door.

"Allison, why don't you take the twins into the kitchen for their surprise," said Dr. Carmichael. "I want to talk with Monica for a brief moment."

"Sure thing, William," she exclaimed.

"Grandma, you have a surprise for us?" asked Brandon looking towards the kitchen.

"I sure do."

"What is it, Grandma?" asked Braylon before his brother could get it out.

"I'm going to bake a home-made apple pie with vanilla ice cream."

"I love apple pie," announced Brandon.

"And vanilla ice cream is my favorite," said his brother.

"Okay, let's go into the kitchen and get started making the pie. You two can help me mix the ingredients."

Off went the twins with their grandmother into the kitchen leaving Monica and her father to their discussion.

"Monica, let's go into my study for a moment so we can talk."

"Sure, dad."

Dr. Carmichael's study was adjacent to the foyer and no one was allowed to enter it unless he was there. The room's longest wall had a hand-crafted bookshelf which contained voluminous rows of books from every imaginable genre. The room also contained a cherry-stained desk where he conducted all his writing and a small lamp was positioned on top of it. In front of the desk were two leather chairs facing one another. He sat in one while his daughter sat quietly in the other.

"Monica, I've been thinking about your future in the last recent weeks," he said finally placing the television remote control on the desk next to his chair.

"What about my future, dad?" she asked crossing her legs in the chair.

"I really want you to give some serious thought about leaving that high school where you teach."

"Dad, we've had this discussion before. There's nothing wrong with me teaching at North Atlanta High School."

"But don't you want something more challenging?"

"What's more challenging than preparing the youth of today to be our leaders for tomorrow?"

"Monica, I guess what I'm trying to say is that I think a career at Emory University would be more rewarding. Besides, you'll be teaching students that already have one foot in the real world."

"Dad, just because I graduated from Emory and you're a professor there doesn't mean I have to teach there too."

"But aren't those kids at the high school level getting a little out of control?"

"No, they are not."

"Monica, just hear me out. There is a vacancy about to come open in the College of Fine Arts at Emory this fall semester. With my influence, I'm sure I can easily get you in."

"This might surprise you but I'm actually happy teaching high school students."

"There's a hefty increase in salary if you move to Emory. Plus, you'll have the opportunity to become tenured later down the road."

"It's not always about the money with me, dad."

"Okay, you've convinced me. I see your mind still hasn't changed a bit from our last conversation. I guess I'm just trying too hard to please daddy's little girl."

"I promise to give it some more thought," said Monica smiling. "But I'm ninety-nine percent sure I'm going to stay put."

As the conversation ended between father and daughter, Monica's mother slowly sticks her head into the study. She is wearing a plaid apron over her clothes and wiping her hands with a red dish cloth.

"Is everything alright in here with you two?" she asked.

"You were right, Allison," said Dr. Carmichael turning his attention towards his wife. "She's not going to budge from leaving her high school for Emory."

"I told you, William, but you had to see for yourself again."

"Listen, I love you two for everything you have done for me," said Monica standing up from her chair. "But I really need to get going if I want to make it to the hair salon on time. Besides, I have to pick up Shanna at her condo downtown."

Monica went over to her dad and gently kissed him on his forehead. Then she did the same to her mother on her cheek. The three departed the study and walked to the kitchen where Brandon and Braylon were busy mixing the ingredients. Monica said good-bye to her sons and headed out the door.

Roughly, fifteen minutes into her drive, Monica made an exit off the Fourteenth Street Bridge headed to Shanna's residence. Shanna lived at Club Tower a once ritzy but now modest high-rise dwelling in downtown Atlanta. Continuing to drive, she noticed it was almost one o'clock and retrieved her cell phone from her purse.

"Come on, Shanna, answer your phone," she said out loud as she placed her cell phone to her ear.

"Hello," said the familiar voice on the other end.

"Hey girl it's Monica."

"Hi, Monica, I was just sitting here waiting for you. Is everything alright?"

"Yeah, it actually took me longer this time to drop the twins off at my parent's house. My dad had to have a one-on-one chat with me again."

"Is he still trying to convince you to leave North Atlanta High School?"

"Yes, Shanna, but I told him I was staying put. Anyway, I'm turning on West Peachtree Street right now. I should be in front of your building in a second."

"Okay that's fine. You can just pull in front of my building and I'll be down shortly. I'm actually walking to the elevator now."

"Sounds good, Shanna. I'll see you in a bit."

West Peachtree has four lanes all traveling in the same direction. Even on Saturday, all lanes were congested with traffic. Somehow, Monica managed to maneuver her vehicle to the far left lane and remained stationary in front of Shanna's building. Then, as promised, Shanna walked through the building's front entrance glass doors, entered the SUV, and the women continued their conversation.

"This traffic downtown is crazy even on the weekends," said Monica pulling the vehicle into merging traffic. "How do you deal with it during the week?"

"It's no big deal to me now," Shanna replied. "I guess I'm use to it."

"So what's the deal with this new hair salon you're taking me to?"

"Monica, you're going to love it. It's called Styles Salon and it's right on Piedmont Road."

"What's the address, Shanna? I can input it into the GPS."

Shanna quickly opened her purse which was in her lap. She found the business card from the salon and pulled it out.

"Ah, here it is," Shanna said holding the card up for Monica to see. "The address is: 2921 Piedmont Road."

"Okay great," said Monica entering the address into the vehicles GPS. "I hope this salon is all the rave you've been speaking about."

"It is and much more. The stylist who did my hair a few weeks ago was awesome!"

"Well, she should be because this is the first time in years I'm letting anyone touch my hair besides my regular hairstylist."

"It will be well worth it just wait and see. And she is actually a he."

"So who is this character, Shanna? I never had a male stylist before."

"His name is Raphael and he's originally from Los Angeles. He told me he has been working at Styles Salon for a few years now."

"Well, at least I like his name. My hair has to be perfect for the twins' birthday party next week."

"Don't worry, Monica, it will be."

CHAPTER 12

By now, the two women finally arrived at Styles Salon in Buckhead. Monica was anxious to find out what all the fuss was about with Shanna's new hair stylist. Even more than that, she hoped this Raphael character would live up to the hype she heard about so far.

After parking in the salon's overcrowded parking lot, the two friends made their way to the front door. Shanna entered first with Monica closely behind her. Upon their entrance, the place was packed for a Saturday afternoon. The first person they saw was the salon's receptionist who was sitting behind an all-glass desk. She was young, pretty, and most importantly smiling.

"Good afternoon, ladies," said the cheerful receptionist as the woman approached her area. "Welcome to Styles Salon my name is Tameka. How can I assist you today?"

"Hello Tameka," said Shanna while Monica glanced around the establishment. "We have an appointment with Raphael today at one o'clock."

"Okay, let me just check our bookings," Tameka said as she moved her fingers along the minicomputer on her desk. "What's your name, ma'am?"

"I'm Shanna Danbury and this is my friend Monica Malone."

"Yes, I've found you two on our system," said Tameka turning her attention back to the woman. "Raphael is still with his client but he should be finished shortly."

"Okay, that's fine," replied Shanna in an eager voice. "We'll wait."

"Feel free to take a seat in our lounge area just to your right," said the friendly receptionist. "There you'll find reading materials and a refreshment bar while you wait."

The two women moved away from Tameka's desk and headed for the lounge area she recommended.

"You're right, Shanna, this is a nice salon," whispered Monica as they continued to walk.

"I told you, Monica. You have to learn to trust me sometimes."

When the women arrived in the seating area they noticed how it was plush, decorated well, and were filled with women waiting for their stylist. Some of the women were flipping through magazines but there was one who was noticeably talking too loud on her cell phone. The pair spotted two empty seats on the oversized chocolate leather sofa in front of them. In addition, sitting on the sofa was a woman patiently waiting with a book in her hand.

"I'm going to grab a beverage at the refreshment bar before I take a seat," said Monica pointing to the bar that was only a few feet away. "Do you want anything from there?"

"No thanks I'm fine. I'll be sure to save you a seat on the sofa."

"I'll be over there soon."

Shanna made her way over to the sofa where the woman was sitting on the end seat. She took the middle seat next to her.

"Hello," said Shanna to the stranger.

"Hi," replied the woman looking at Shanna briefly and then quickly focused her attention back to the book she was reading.

"Sorry, I couldn't help but notice the illustration cover to the book in your hand. Is that an older title you're reading?"

"Actually no," answered the woman turning her attention back to Shanna. "It's a fairly new book I think the author just used a retro look for the book cover."

"Who's the author?"

"He's an up-and-coming author named Frederick Germaine. The book is called *Ladies' Man*."

"*Ladies' Man!*" shouted Shanna. "I don't think I'll be recommending that title to my book club any time soon. The last thing we want to read is a book about a womanizing man."

"It's really pretty good so far," said the woman continuing the dialogue. "The author depicts a male-perception storyline where the man's heart is actually broken by his cheating girlfriend. That alone compels him to try his fate at being a ladies' man."

"Oh, well, that sounds interesting and different."

By now, Monica joined the pair with her beverage in hand. She sat next to Shanna on the leather sofa. The other woman immersed herself back into the book she was reading.

"So what did you get to drink?" asked Shanna turning to her friend.

"A cappuccino," replied Monica taking a sip from her cup.

Before the two could continue their conversation, up walks a man to the sofa. He stood at least six-four and weighed two hundred and thirty pounds. His biceps and chest protruded through the tight-fitting shirt he was wearing.

"Shanna, is that you again?" asked the tall well built man.

"Raphael!" shouted out Shanna as she stood up to greet him. "Yes, I decided to come back and this time I brought my friend."

"Well, bless your heart, honey. Now give me a hug and a kiss because it's so good to see you again."

Shanna eagerly complied and gave Raphael a friendly hug. Then he turned his cheek to hers and gave her a kiss without actually kissing her. He repeated the process to her other cheek.

"And who is this cute little button with you?" he asked.

"Raphael, this is my good friend, Monica."

Not knowing what to expect, Monica stood up, smiled bashfully, and extended her hand out to him.

"Oh girl, give me a hug and a kiss too," he said in his friendly tone. "We're all family up in here."

The two hugged and Raphael kissed both sides of Monica's cheek as he did with Shanna. After that, the two separated.

"You two can follow me back to my work area. There's an extra chair for Monica to sit in while I begin on your hair first, Shanna."

Both women followed Raphael as the rest of the women in the lounge area looked on. As the three walked through the salon, they passed an array of beautiful woman being given a distinctive look only Atlanta was known for. But no other stylish in the salon could compete with Raphael. Hands down he was the best.

"Well, here we are ladies," said Raphael once they reached his work area.

He had three full-size salon chairs in his area with floor-to-ceiling mirrors in front of each. The area was spacious and neat. Behind each chair was a black opiate colored sink and a hair dryer. Shanna took a seat right next to where Raphael stood as Monica positioned herself in one of the remaining chairs.

"So what's the occasion this time," asked Raphael as he effortlessly combed his fingers through Shanna's hair. "You have another hot date?"

"Hell no," yelled Shanna looking frustrated.

"Shanna!" screamed Monica as her friend's answer caught her off guard.

"I'm so sorry, Monica. But I'm so sick and tired of these men in Atlanta. All they want is sex, sex, and more sex."

"Darling, I just love these sexy men in Atlanta," responded Raphael in a flamboyant tone. "I don't know what I'd do without them."

"Very funny, Raphael," said Shanna. "But that's easy for you to say. Lately, my friend, I keep in the nightstand, has been my best comfort."

"Oh, girl, I'm scared of you," blurted out Raphael.

"Well, don't be Raphael because there's no shame in my game. It will have to suffice until I find Mr. Right."

"So darling you want it the same way as last time?" asked Raphael as he placed a cape over Shanna's body.

"I guess so Raphael. I really liked the new look you gave me."

"How about if I jazz it up even a bit more and cut the ends then add some highlights?"

"I think I'll like that even more."

"Girl, after I finish with you, you're going to look like a knockout."

"Well, maybe somebody will notice at the party next Saturday," Shanna said in an excited manner.

"What party?" asked Raphael.

"My husband and I are celebrating our twins' birthday," interjected Monica.

"Oh, how sweet, Monica," said Raphael. "So how old will they be?"

"They are turning four," she replied back.

"Yeah and Monica promised there would be a few eligible bachelors from her husband's company at the party," Shanna said with confidence.

"I promise those men are going to fight over you," Raphael stated. "But first we need to get you under the sink for a wash."

l

PART II

THE UNEXPECTED GUEST

CHAPTER 13

"Dammit this woman is going to kill me," said Sebastian to himself as he looked at his watch. "It's already nine-thirty and I was supposed to be at her house at eight."

He exits the elevator on the floor of the high-rise where his date for the evening resides. Boastfully, he walks down the narrow hallway passing countless doors with a bouquet of fresh flowers in his hand. Managing to find a florist open this late on a Saturday night was no easy task, but easy enough for him. The flowers would surely comfort his date's anger he assumed.

"I think this is it," he speaks to himself again pausing in front of a door in the hallway. "I hate this high-rise, all the doors on every floor look alike and I always forget her suite number."

Calmly, he takes a deep breath, gathers his composure, and then gently knocks on the door. After no answer, he repeats the process but this time knocking a little louder. Finally, on the other end of the door he hears the deadbolt turning and the door opens.

"Oh, I'm sorry I must have knocked on the wrong residence," said Sebastian looking at the woman in front of him.

The woman had pried the door open just enough where he could get a glimpse of her. She was beautiful, dressed in a provocative red negligee showing a little bit of her goodies, and barefoot too.

"Well, maybe I can help you find her," said the mysterious woman eyeballing him up and down. "What does she look like?"

"She's about your height, physique, and very attractive just like you."

"Sorry mister, I don't recall anyone on this floor resembling my looks. You might want to try another floor."

"That's too bad, I kind of wish I was lost on purpose now."

"Are you flirting with me, mister?"

"Only if it would get you to open the door a bit wider so I could get to know you better."

"No, I don't think so. Besides, my boyfriend who is real jealous is on his way over."

Abruptly and rudely, the mysterious woman slams the door in front of Sebastian's face before he could mutter another word out of his mouth. Dejected, he pauses while looking at the flowers he still held in his hand. Then he turns and walks away slowly. Suddenly, the door where the woman once stood opens up again.

"Sebastian, you better get in here," she softly announces while peaking her head outside the door.

With his back towards the door and halfway down the hallway he cracks an enormous smile. Then he turns around keeping his smile and opens his arms up to the woman who just closed the door on him a few seconds ago.

"Baby, did you miss me?" he asked once he arrived back at the front of the door again.

The woman grabs him by the front of his shirt and yanks him into her residence. She instantly pushes him onto the wall and closes the front door.

"Did I?" she asked not letting him answer. Then she kisses him frantically on his lips and moves down to his neck while rubbing his muscular chest. "I hate it when you're always late. What took you so long?"

"Just another mundane Saturday at the office trying to meet a deadline," he replied. "Sorry, baby, I simply lost track of time. But look I brought these for you."

He hands her the bouquet of flowers that are still grasped in his hand. Hopefully, they will make up for the lost time.

"They're beautiful, Sebastian," she said taking the flowers from his hand. Then she playfully strikes him on his shoulder with the same flowers. "I swear I'm going to kill you the next time you're late. Dinner has been ready for almost two hours now."

"I'm sorry, baby."

"I forgive you this time. Now take a seat at the table while I put these flowers in some water."

The round table was already set to display a romantic theme for the couple. A well pressed white linen tablecloth draped over the table all the way down to the floor. On top of the table, sat two slender candles displayed in a sterling finished holder. Next to the table was a bottle of wine being chilled in an elegant bucket.

"So what are we having for dinner?" he asked while taking a seat at the decked out table as instructed.

"T-bone steaks cooked medium rare just the way you liked them served with sauté onions on top. Plus, I made sweet potatoes, steamed broccoli, and a fresh chef salad with all the extras."

"That sounds delicious but I wouldn't mind tasting something else first."

"Oh, no you don't, Sebastian. You're going to have to wait just like I had to wait on you."

"Come on, baby, don't keep me waiting. How about giving me a little appetizer before the main meal?"

"No. Besides, it took a lot of time and energy preparing this meal for us to enjoy."

"Okay you win."

While Sebastian patiently waits for his meal to arrive, his date for the evening meanders throughout the kitchen. She finally arrives placing the bouquet of flowers, in a vase halfway filled with water, at the center of the table. Afterwards, she returns to the kitchen then back to the table with their plates.

"Baby, this looks scrumptious," said Sebastian looking down at his plate she places in front of him. "You cooked all this yourself?"

"Yes, I did."

"Looks like all the effort you put into those cooking classes have paid off."

"Well, don't just sit there admiring it tell me how it tastes," she said lighting the two candles and taking a seat across from him.

He unfolds his fork and knife from his linen napkin and cuts into the juicy steak but not before he tops it with A1 Steak Sauce. After cutting a large portion, he places it into his mouth onions and all.

"Hmmm, baby that's so good," he said with his mouth half full of steak.

"I'm glad you like it," she said beginning to carefully run the tines of her fork over her steam broccoli. "So how are things going at work?"

"Work is work."

"What about the promotion you've been talking about?"

"I've been working very diligently lately. I think eventually my boss will see things my way."

Sebastian rises from his seat and retrieves the chilled bottle of wine that waits nearby. He uncorks the bottle and fills his date's wine glass half-full. Then he pours himself an equal amount and replaces the bottle back into the bucket.

"Let's make a toast," he summoned holding up his wine glass while standing.

His date eagerly jumps to her feet with wine glass in hand and joins him near his seat.

"So what are we toasting to, Sebastian?"

"We're toasting to us, our future, and everything we worked so hard for."

The two make their wine glasses meet which gave off a soft chime sound. Then it was bottoms up for him. He gently grabs her at the base of her neck and has a handful of her hair in the process.

"Be careful, Sebastian, I just left the hair salon earlier today."

"Well, your hair is sure to get messed up now."

Without haste, he blows the lit candles out which were slowly burning. In a violent manner he shoves everything off the table.

"Sebastian, what the hell are you doing?" she screams out.

"Sit on top of the table now!" he orders her.

"And what if I don't?"

"Dammit, I said sit your sexy ass on top of the table."

"Oh, I just love it when you take the aggressive tone with me. It's such a turn on."

While she complied with his wishes, he took the glass from her hand and set it aside with his out the way. Quickly, he removed his shirt showing off his gridiron physique. She leaned back on her elbows giving herself support. Before he could say another word, she spread open her legs giving him what he was looking for since he came through the door.

"Yeah, that's how I like you to spread those legs," he said getting excited. "Now take a deep breath because I'm about to go down on you like a parachute."

He teases her first by gently kissing only her bellybutton and rubs her clitoris with his thumb. Slowly, he inches closer to her hot spot with his tongue while she closes her eyes. As he finally allows his wet tongue to massage her clitoris, she places one of her legs on his shoulder.

"Oh, Sebastian, that feels so good," she moans out placing her remaining free leg on his other shoulder.

"Uh huh," he added still pleasing her with his magic tongue.

After she was all worked up, he then took the top of his tongue and positioned it at the base of her vagina. He licked upwards being careful to move slowly and massage her pussy lips in the process. He ended up back on her clitoris nibbling it a bit this time. He repeated this process over, and over, and over again until her legs began to tremble like an earthquake on his shoulders.

"Shit!" she cried out with her head fully extended back. "I want you inside of me."

"I thought you'd never ask."

His tongue had been in overdrive and her wet pussy was spewing with juices he loved to taste. He finally came up for air and placed her legs off his shoulders but carefully arched on the table. Then he unbuckled his belt, unzipped his pants, and a long hard thick dick fell out. She managed to gain some sort of composure now and turned her head forward to see what was in front of her. Just as she did, he maneuvered his arms up under her legs where the palm of his huge hands rested on top of her thighs. Suddenly, he inched her closer to him for greater leverage.

"Here it comes inside of you, baby," he said while placing himself in her without using his hands.

"I thought it couldn't be this good again," she winched out.

Their two bodies stuck together like molasses and only spread apart long enough for him to thrust deeper. She caresses his strokes making sure she felt every inch of him. As she now moans in pleasure, he's pleased she is being satisfied at the moment. She gets wetter and his dick even seems to get harder as the strokes turn into pounding. The sounds of their wet bodies clashing makes Sebastian turn up the heat even more. He finally gets there, but not before she does. Breathing as if they just ran a marathon, the two remained positioned on the edge of the table as if they were posing for a sculpture's masterpiece. Neither one of them could say a word. There was just a calm, yet continuous, exhale from the two. While beneath them, the floor was still littered with the dinner décor.

CHAPTER 14

"Mommy and daddy wake up!" screamed Brandon running into our bedroom as fast as he could. "It's our birthday!"

By the time his feet reached the edge of our king-size bed, he took one giant leap as if he was a gymnast and flopped into our bed. Amazingly, he landed between Monica and I who were still trying to sleep.

"Brandon, what are you doing up so early?" asked Monica with her eyes still closed as she lay in the bed.

Still lying on my side with my back to her and Brandon, I reached over to the nightstand and picked up my cell phone. I was dreading to see what time it was.

"Monica, it's only seven-thirty," I said in a sleepy tone.

"Brandon, grown-ups are supposed to sleep in late on Saturday mornings," she said finally opening her eyes and looking at her son.

"I know, mommy, but it's our birthday."

"Here I come, mommy!" yelled Braylon running down the hall and entering our bedroom now.

Just as his brother did a few moments before him, he gave his best impression of an acrobat and flipped into our bed landing next to his brother. Only this time, he raised his hands, laughed, and smiled as if we were judges at a contest.

"Happy birthday, boys," said Monica rising up in the bed as she hugged the twins.

"Daddy, wake up," said Brandon as he nudged my back.

"I'm up, I'm up," I said rolling over and facing the trio. "You two birthday boys come over here and give your daddy a kiss."

The twins did as they were told. First Brandon kissed me on the cheek and as always Braylon followed him.

"Where are our presents?" asked Brandon turning his attention back to his mother.

"Yeah, we want to open our gifts," said his brother.

"Oh, no you two," Monica said. "You'll have to wait until this afternoon at your birthday party. All your friends are coming over with all kinds of gifts."

"No, mommy, I can't wait that long," pouted Brandon as he folded his arms and frowned in his Spider Man pajamas.

As Brandon pleaded his case with Monica, I rose to my feet and walked to one of the three windows closest to our bed. The Saturday sun was barley trickling into the room and I figured I'd open the wooden blinds. Once I did, I noticed a white utility van parked next door in our neighbor's driveway. The black lettering on the van read: Ace Security Systems. 'No job is too big or too small' was their motto written directly under the company's name.

"Looks like Mrs. Chastain, our next door neighbor, is having some new work done to her security system," I said wiping the sleep out of my eyes.

"I guess she feels you can never be too cautious," Monica stated turning her attention away from the twins briefly.

"Yeah, I guess you're right."

Ms. Chastain was in her mid-seventies and had been a widow for nearly ten years now. She was the first person to welcome us into the neighborhood when we purchased our house after the wedding. Her favorite pastime was baking and she revealed this to us by delivering a homemade red-velvet cake as a house warming gift. We had even invited her to the twins' birthday party hoping she would bring over some sweet goodies. Ironically, her husband had retired from the now-defunct General Motors assembly plant before he died.

"So you two really want to open your gifts now?" Monica asked catering to the twins wishes.

"Yeah!" screamed both of them together at the top of their lungs.

"Okay, let's go and see what's in store for you two downstairs."

Monica's body emerged from beneath the covers as the excited twins' feet hit the floor before hers did. Little did the twins know that downstairs there were two brand new shiny blue bicycles they so desperately wanted.

I worked late last night at the office making amendments for the revitalization project. After that, I drove to Toys R Us and picked up the assembled gifts. It was a hassle trying to fit both bikes into my Audi but somehow I managed. Fortunately for me, the twins were sound asleep when I made it home.

"Are you coming, Aaron?" Monica asked as I still stood by the window.

"You guys go ahead I'll be down in a minute."

"Come on, mommy, let's go," Brandon impatiently requested tugging on his mother's arm.

"Okay, here I come," she said as Braylon grabbed her other arm.

"So what time did you say the bounce house company is coming by to set up?" I asked Monica before they all headed out the room.

"Aaron, that was supposed to be a surprise!"

"Oops. Well, surprise boys."

"We get to play on a bounce house at our party today, daddy?" asked Brandon.

"Yup that's right," I said. "It's for both of you and all your friends who are coming over."

"Honey, the bounce house company should arrive an hour before the party begins," Monica said. "And my parents should be here well before then."

"Okay. Now you better get going downstairs before those two yank your arms off."

While Monica and the twins ran off downstairs, I moved to the bathroom where I slapped some cold water on my face then brushed my teeth. As I looked up from the bathroom sink into the mirror, I noticed a few strains of grey hair starting to show on the side of my head.

"You're starting to get old, Aaron," I said to myself in the mirror while chuckling. "I guess we all do sooner or later."

Then I grabbed my wool robe, placed it on, and secured the belt around my waist. It was now time to head downstairs and watch my boys have some fun.

"Daddy, look I'm riding my bike," Brandon said while zipping past me once I made it downstairs.

"Me too, see," said his brother closely following behind him on his new bike.

The twins were riding their bikes in a circular motion in the area between the kitchen and living room. The training wheels on the bikes kept their balance while the hardwood floor gave them the traction to keep them moving.

"Hey, you two are going to destroy something in here," I said watching them make circles around me. "How about we go outside in the driveway for a test drive?"

"Okay daddy," announced Brandon while his brother continued to follow him on his bike.

"Don't be too long," said Monica while peaking her head from the kitchen looking at the three of us. "Breakfast will be ready in a few minutes. And make sure they wear their helmets, Aaron."

"Mommy, I don't need to wear a helmet," Brandon said pausing for a minute and folding his arms again as he did earlier in our bed. "I'm a big boy now."

"Well, big boys still need to wear helmets too, Brandon," I said while I went into the living room to retrieve the head gear.

I was able to pry both of them off their bikes long enough so I could carry both bikes out of the house. Once we were outside, I fitted both twins with their helmets and they quickly repositioned themselves on their bikes. This time they had more than enough room to ride.

"Now, stay in the driveway and don't go out in the street," I said firmly to both of them.

"Okay," replied the two of them as they took off.

As I watched the twins continue to enjoy their bike ride, out strolls our next-door neighbor, Mrs. Chastain. She was already dressed for the day in aqua colored pants and a white blouse. Her hair, which was grey all over, was perfectly styled as always.

"Good morning, Aaron," she said as she waved from her porch standing outside her front door. Her other hand was placed around a crystal coffee cup.

"Good morning to you, Mrs. Chastain," I replied back feeling somewhat awkward as I stood in the driveway with my hands in my robe's pocket.

"I see the twins are out enjoying their birthday gift," she said then takes a sip of coffee from her cup. "Happy birthday, twins."

"Hi Mrs. Chastain," said the twins together without looking up.

"So, Aaron, is the twins' birthday party still set for two o'clock today?"

"Yes ma'am. We look forward to seeing you there with some of your tasty desserts."

"I'm in the kitchen now trying to decide what to bake and bring over."

"Well, whatever you decide we know it's going to be good," I said. "So is everything alright with your security system this morning?"

"Oh yes, dear. I'm just having my security system upgraded a bit. You know how a little old woman like me can get spooked easily."

"Don't be Mrs. Chastain. You know Monica and I are always just a few feet away."

"That's mighty sweet of you, Aaron. Well, I think I hear the security guy calling for me. I'll see you all later this afternoon."

"See you soon, Mrs. Chastain."

For a few more minutes, the surprised twins continued to enjoy their bikes. Once I got a whiff of Monica's cooking penetrating the front door, I knew it was time to go. Only the twins were disappointed we had to go back inside.

Back inside the home we all sat down at the breakfast table. Monica's cooking hit the spot for my growling stomach. The twins hardly touched their food overly excited about the day still to come. After breakfast, we all went back upstairs to get prepared for the long day ahead of us.

It was noon when Monica and I started hanging the twins' birthday decorations. We were on the wooden deck which extended on the ground from our house in the back yard. Near us the twins were busy kicking their new soccer ball to each other in the freshly cut green lawn. They managed to convince their mother to allow them to open another one of their gifts before the party officially began. Suddenly, the front door bell rang which caused us to pause.

"Sounds like our first guest have arrived," I said as I finished tying a ribbon to the end of a blue colored balloon.

"It's probably my parents," Monica replied back. "I'll go get the door."

"Oh no, sweetheart, you have been working way too hard already so far. Just stay put I'll go get it."

"Okay Aaron."

Monica stayed behind completing the Happy Feet cartoon character theme that the twins so desperately wanted for their party. I dashed back inside the house, passing the living room and kitchen, and then finally made it to the front door. Just as Monica predicted, it was her parents standing there once I opened the door.

"Dr. Carmichael and Allison, we figured it was you two at the door. Come on in."

"Hello there, Aaron," said Allison walking into our home with her arms held outwards for a hug. "How have you been doing?"

"I've been good," I said hugging her. "And how have you been?"

"Oh, you know me as good as I'll ever be."

After our brief embrace, Dr. Carmichael followed his wife into the house. He was carrying two medium sized boxes which were carefully gift wrapped but it didn't prevent him from extending his right hand to me.

"Aaron, glad to finally see you again," he said giving me a firm handshake. "How's the revitalization project going?"

"It's coming along very well."

"I'm glad to hear that."

"So how is everything over at Emory?" I asked him.

"It couldn't be better," he replied back quickly.

"Now, where are the birthday boys?" asked Allison as I closed the front door. "I couldn't wait to get over here today and see their cute little faces."

"They're in the back yard playing with their new soccer ball," I said. "Monica and I are just finishing up with the decorations. Come on in and follow me."

After our brief exchange of greetings, my in-laws followed me to the rear of the house. They were excited to see the back yard where Monica and the twins were.

"Grandma and grandpa," yelled the twins as they noticed the pair from the middle of the back yard.

Their grandmother was the first to meet them. She bent down on one knee and graciously opened her arms for the twins who hugged her without hesitation.

"Happy birthday, boys," she said still embracing them.

"Are those our presents?" Brandon asked while pointing to the gifts his grandfather was carrying.

"Yes, they are," replied Dr. Carmichael placing the gifts on a large table nearby on the wooden deck. The same table was reserved for the twins' birthday gifts. "But you'll have to wait until the party begins before you can open them. Now, come over here and give your grandpa a hug."

Their grandmother reluctantly rose to her feet letting the twins go. Dr. Carmichael mimicked his wife and bent down too, hugging his grandchildren. By now, Monica had made it over to where her parents were and exchanged hugs with them too.

"Now, this is the other thing I've been dying to get my hands on today," said Dr. Carmichael looking at the stainless-steel grill next to him.

What drew his attention was the Viking professional grill which stood out like a sore thumb. It was a mammoth of a grill and measured six-feet in length, four-feet high, and three feet in width. It had a well-ventilated grilling area, wet bar, cooler, and any other modern-day amenities any chef would drool over. I purchased the grill a month earlier knowing it would come in handy on a day like this.

"Monica, your father has been talking about that grill ever since we woke up this morning," Allison said.

"Mom, you know dad loves to show off his cooking skills on the grill. I even remember him grilling at my birthday parties."

"You both know it's all about the smoke and my secret sauce when it comes to my grilling technique," said Dr. Carmichael. "The smoke slowly cooks the meat and adds flavor while the sauce adds an extra punch. And I only grill with hickory wood never charcoal."

"I have you all covered, Dr. Carmichael," I said interjecting my two cents. "The grill has a rear compartment supply of hickory, birch, and oak wood."

"Well done, Aaron," he said. "Now, all I need is an apron."

"Enough said," I replied. "Just follow me into the kitchen and I'll get you all squared away."

"Yeah dad, Aaron and I even marinated the meat in seasoning the night before. It's waiting for you in the refrigerator."

"I see you still remembered, Monica," said Dr. Carmichael.

"Oh, William, how could she forget?" said his wife. "You practically taught her everything about grilling before she was five."

Dr. Carmichael expressed a wide grin on his face that was followed up with a short laugh. Then everyone followed suit and laughed with him. I led him into the kitchen while Monica and her mother worked on finalizing the decorations throughout the back yard. And the twins went back to kicking their soccer ball among themselves.

CHAPTER 15

By three o'clock the twins' birthday party was in full swing. My colleagues from work had arrived along with Monica's too. As Raphael predicted, Shanna had her hands full with a few of my male co-workers who were impressed by her new look. Even I noticed a glow about her. As promised, Jane arrived and brought her grandchildren who blended in well with the other kids. Even Mrs. Chastain showed up with double-layered German chocolate cake and chocolate-chip cookies.

The mood was festive in the backyard as Dr. Carmichael was taking the last portion of franks, burgers, and barbeque chicken coated with his secret sauce off the grill. All the kids were preoccupied jumping around in the bounce house and didn't notice the food was ready. As I looked around admiring how enjoyable the afternoon was turning out the front doorbell rang again.

"I got it," I shouted over the crowd noise as if anyone was even paying attention to my remark.

I had been the designated door greeter for much of the day. It seemed like this had to be my fiftieth trip to the front door. Like before, I gladly made the quick run. When I arrived and opened the door, there stood a very familiar face on the other end.

"Sebastian, you finally made it," I said smiling at my good friend.

"Yeah, Aaron, you know me and punctuality are never on the same page, especially when it comes to birthday parties."

"Ah, come on, you know it's no big deal. The fun has just begun. Come on in and join us in the back yard."

Sebastian had a fairly large gift under his right arm but his stature made it seem smaller. His body reeked of light pleasant-smelling cologne and he was dressed well for the occasion.

"Well, aren't you looking spiffy, today," I said as he entered the house. "And you smell good too."

"Oh, it's just something I tossed together at the last moment. I'm actually reconnecting with an old acquaintance later on today that's why you smell the new cologne."

"The life of an eligible bachelor it must keep you on your toes."

"Yeah, you know how it is," he said grinning showing his perfect white teeth. "Oh, well, I guess you don't."

By the time we made it halfway through the house on our way to the back yard, Shanna appeared. We all three crossed each other's path at the kitchen.

"There you are, Aaron," Shanna said pretending not to even notice Sebastian. "I came in here to get some mustard."

"Did we run out already?" I asked.

"Apparently so," she replied. "You know how kids love mustard on their franks."

"There's an extra container of mustard on the third shelf in the pantry right next to the refrigerator."

Shanna followed my directions and moved over to the pantry seeking the mustard. Sebastian eyebrows rose as he noticed her sexy dress and new look.

"Well, hello Shanna. I haven't seen you in a while," he said in a pleasant tone.

"Hi, Sebastian," she said with more interest in finding the mustard as she rose on her toes looking on the third shelf in the pantry. "Ah, I found it."

"I see you've been keeping in shape," he said with his eyes fixed on her backside.

After retrieving the container of mustard, Shanna calmly and collectively walked right up to Sebastian. She stopped once she was no more than six inches from his face.

"Look, Sebastian, we don't get along and let's keep it that way," she said slightly looking up at him in a matter of fact way. "Let's just pretend we do in front of these guests. Once the party is over you can go on your way and I'll go mine."

"Some things never changed from Aaron's wedding," he said in disgust. "Especially you and that damn attitude of yours."

"You two stop it already with your quarreling and I mean it!" I said trying to keep the peace between two people who hated each other. "If I didn't know any better I'd say you two were having a love spat."

"Aaron, please believe me when I say this," Shanna said turning her face to me. "Sebastian and I will never be together."

Shanna twisted her body in a one-hundred and eighty-degree turn towards the direction she previously came from. With the container of mustard tightly in her hand she headed for the back yard.

"Gee whiz talk about someone needing to get some," mumbled Sebastian under his breath as he continued to look at her backside. "I guess some things will never change."

"Come on, Sebastian, forget about it. Let's get you to the back yard and introduced to everyone."

When we arrived in the back yard, Shanna had already given the kids the container of mustard they were anxiously waiting for. Then she disappeared into a thick crowd of women making small talk.

"Sebastian, there you are," shouted Monica over the crowd noise and appearing to our left. She greeted him with a friendly hug. "It's so good to see you again."

"It's a pleasure to see you as well, Monica."

"I see you've brought the twins a pretty nice size birthday gift."

"Well, nothing is too big or small for my favorite boys," he said looking throughout the crowd in the back yard. "Where are they anyway? I want to give them their gift."

"Good luck with that. They're playing inside the bounce house with a few of their friends and refuse to come out."

Monica pointed in the direction to where the bounce house was set up. Inside, the twins and their friends were jumping up and down yelling at the top of their lungs.

"Okay, I see what you mean," he said. "They are definitely having a blast."

Before the conversation between the two of them could continue the front doorbell rang again. All three of us slightly turned our heads to the sound. I wasn't surprised a bit as I had been playing the role of a butler all day long.

"I'll get it, sweetheart," I said to my wife.

"No, I'll get it this time, honey," she said. "You've been answering the door all day anyway. And my dad is anxious to get another person to taste his secret signature barbeque sauce."

"Did you say barbeque, Monica?" Sebastian asked while his eyes peeked with interest.

"Yes, my dad loves to cook especially his favorite dish which is barbeque chicken. He even thought about applying for a patent for his so-called world-famous sauce."

"Well, lead the way, Aaron," said Sebastian licking his lips. "I can't wait to taste his barbeque and neither can my stomach."

Then the doorbell rang again as it seemed like the person was getting impatient. Like previously, we all turned our heads slightly to the sound.

"You better get the front door before our anxious guest decides to leave," I said to Monica.

"Yes, Aaron, I'm on my way. Oh, it's just one other thing I have to tell you, Sebastian."

"What's that?"

"The gift table for the twins is next to the barbeque grill. You can place your present there."

"Okay Monica," said Sebastian as the doorbell rang for a third time.

"Sweetheart, the front door awaits you," I said looking at my wife.

"Okay, okay, okay I'm going. I'll talk with you guys in a minute."

Monica walked briskly to the front door wondering who the anxious guest was. She quickly stroked her hand though her hair to make sure it was still immaculate as it had been all day long. Once she arrived at the front door, she eagerly turned the knob.

"Hello there," Monica said to the stranger as she fully opened the front door.

The attractive stranger was a woman about her height in a light pink pastel-colored dress. Her dress was conservative yet trendy enough to catch everyone's attention. She even wore a pair of matching expensive high-end heels to compliment her outfit. In her hand, there was a small box that was gift wrapped.

"Hi, you must be Monica," said the stranger with a Catholic smile.

"Why yes I am."

"I'm Tiffany Towns. I worked with your husband, Aaron, on the revitalization project."

"Oh, yes Tiffany, it's so good to finally put a face with a name. Please come on in."

Tiffany complied and easily walked into the house. Once inside the two women continued their conversation.

"So Aaron finally decided to invite you, anyway?"

"Yes he did," Tiffany replied maintaining the perfect grin on her face. "I hope you didn't mind."

"No not at all, Tiffany. He was reluctant at first to extend an invitation to you but I suggested he invite you anyway."

"Well, good for you Monica."

"So what do we have here?" Monica asked looking at the present in Tiffany's hand.

"This is just a small gift I brought over for the twins," Tiffany said handing the box to her.

"Tiffany, you didn't have to go through the trouble of buying a gift."

"It was no trouble at all, Monica. Besides, your sons are supposed to receive gifts on their birthday."

"Thanks for the kind gesture. I'm sure they will enjoy it."

"Anytime, now where are those two handsome boys of yours?

They're in the back yard having a ball," answered Monica as she secured the gift in her possession. "Follow me so you can meet them and everyone else."

The two women departed from the front of the house and made their way towards the rear. Their walk was slow but steady.

"Your home is beautifully designed and decorated," commented Tiffany during their walk.

"Thank you, Tiffany," said Monica in a prideful way. "Aaron fell in love with the house the first time we saw it. I did the interior designing all by myself."

"I see you definitely have a knack for that. Is that something you do professionally?"

"I only wished. I actually teach at North Atlanta High School."

"That's a rewarding career in itself, Monica. Your school has excelled in academics and achievements for years."

"Well someone needs to explain that to my dad because he's been trying to get me to leave the school."

"And go where?"

"Over to Emory University where he is a professor."

After their short talk, the women finally reached the back yard. It was consumed with laughter, music, and joyous noise as when Monica had left it earlier.

Sebastian had been introduced, by Aaron, to Dr. Carmichael and was now stuffing his face with barbeque chicken. The three men were huddled up around the grill enjoying each other. Sebastian nervously placed the barbeque chicken from his mouth onto the paper plate that rested in his other hand. Then he tugged on Aaron's arm moving him out of hearing distance from Dr. Carmichael.

"Aaron, do you see what I see?"

"Yeah, I see everybody having a good time."

"No, that's not what I mean. Look over there towards the door leading back into the house."

As Sebastian had pointed out, it was Monica and Tiffany who had now entered the back yard. Monica still carried the small gift in her arms while she introduced the new guest to everyone in their path. Slowly, they were making their way towards the men.

"Now, you're either one brave man or simply trying to get killed by your wife," Sebastian said taking another bite out of his barbeque chicken. "Which one is it?"

"What the hell!" I shouted softly trying not to get Dr. Carmichael to notice. "What is she doing here?"

"It seems like she's getting to know your wife pretty well."

"Shit, Sebastian, I didn't invite her let alone tell her where I lived."

"Well, you better get over there and straighten things out before all hell breaks loose."

Before Sebastian could say another word, I made my way over to my wife and Tiffany. Tiffany saw me coming and had a silly and smirkish grin on her face but concealed it from my wife.

"Honey, there you are," said Monica as I approached. "Look who showed up."

"Tiffany, what a pleasant surprise to see you," I said smiling hiding my disappointment behind my grin.

"Nice to see you once again, too, Aaron," Tiffany replied in a patronizing way.

"And she even brought the twins a birthday gift," said Monica handing me the wrapped box as I turned my attention to her.

"We thank you for the thought," I said taking the gift. "I'm sure the twins will find it amusing."

"You're quite welcome, Aaron." Tiffany said maintaining an innocent look on her face. "I'm pretty sure they will."

"Honey, why don't you go place the gift on the table with the other items," my wife said to me. "I want to introduce Tiffany to our guests before we sing happy birthday to the twins and cut the cake."

"Sure thing, sweetheart," I said reluctantly.

I stood there with an unnoticeable dumbfounded look on my face. It was awkward to see my wife and the woman I had an affair with so cordial. However, I knew right now Monica had no idea what when on between Tiffany and I. The both of them walked away as I made my way over to the gift table.

For what seemed like eternity, I watched Monica introduce Tiffany to our guests. Tiffany kept her composure as if nothing was wrong and that alone made the rage build up inside me. Finally, Tiffany broke away from Monica and headed back inside the house. I figured she was headed to the powder room and this would be a good time to intervene. Without being obvious, I quickly raced behind her.

"What on God's green earth are you doing here? I shouted halting Tiffany in her tracks. "And how did you find out where I lived?"

Tiffany had made it all the way to the powder room which was near the front door entrance. She paused but didn't turn around.

"I thought my departure from your wife would get your attention," she said turning around facing me. "You'd be surprised what I could find on your secretary's computer once she left it unattended."

I grabbed Tiffany by her elbow and maneuvered her near the door that exited to the garage. So our voices couldn't be heard, I pushed her into the garage and closed the door behind us. The garage was partially dark and only lit by the beans of sunlight passing through the side of the garage door.

"Listen here you crazy lunatic," I said grabbing her around the throat. "I want you out of my house, now!"

"Aaron, you're getting rough with me again and you know that turns me on."

I visually caught a glimpse of myself around her neck. Then I let her go and slightly pushed her backwards.

"Tiffany, you have no right to be here and I mean that. I'm walking out this garage and back to the birthday party. When I get there I expect you to be gone."

"Oh, come on now, don't be such a party pooper. Doesn't this garage remind you of something?"

"Hell no!"

"It's dark, steamy, and hot in here just like it was at my place when we made love."

"It was just one night of kinky sex, Tiffany."

Tiffany advanced towards me and grabbed my right hand placing it on her breasts. Then she slowly moved my middle finger over her harden nipples.

"Come on, Aaron, let me suck you off. I want to see that gratifying expression on your face again."

"You're sick," I said as she still had control of my hand.

"Heck, I'll even let you recline back in your wife's car. It's the Tahoe, right?"

"Get the fuck out of here!" I screamed as I jerked my hand off her breasts. "You have two minutes to leave."

When I returned to the back yard, the crowd had assembled to watch the cake ceremony. I had left Tiffany in the garage and firmly slammed the door behind me. In front of the crowd, Monica had lit the candle that was in the shape of the number four. The candle was placed squarely in the center of the cake with the traditional writing 'happy birthday' on it. I took my place in front of the cake where the twins and Monica were.

"Happy birthday!" yelled everyone in the crowd as the twins blew out the candle together.

The crowd clapped exuberantly, smiled, and showered the twins with praises. I then kissed both of my sons on their cheek knowing they would remember this day forever. When I looked up and towards the rear of the crowd, there stood Tiffany. She was clapping along with the crowd. And she had a silly and smirkish grin on her face that I saw before.

CHAPTER 16

The final bell for the afternoon class rang as it was the last day for seniors at North Atlanta High School. Wildly enough, the seniors left their classrooms and quickly filled the halls. There they littered loose sheets of paper until the floors were not visible. It's a harmless tradition they had performed with only the school's custodian getting angry with the cleanup that followed.

Instead of heading to the school's parking lot and joining the rest of the seniors for a brief celebration, Marilyn made her way down to Monica's room. The graduation ceremonies and the Memorial Day weekend were in a few days and she wanted to say her final good-byes to her English teacher. After she made it past the cluttered fill halls, she noticed Monica was inside her room. Monica was packing her small leather bag with her laptop and books about to depart for the day.

"Mrs. Malone I'm glad I caught you before you left."

"Hi, Marilyn," Monica said pausing from packing her bag. "I thought you'd be outside by now with your classmates."

"No, I figured I do something more important."

"Oh yeah, what's that?"

"I just wanted to tell you how much of an inspiration you had been to me this year. And to come by and thank you personally."

"Marilyn that's so sweet for you to say that. It really means a lot to me."

The two embraced in a warm and thoughtful hug while smiling. It was the intangible times like these when Monica knew her father would never understand why she loved teaching where she did.

"You deserve it, Mrs. Malone," Marilyn said as the two separated from their hug.

"And you deserved to be named senior class valedictorian. Vanderbilt University is gaining such an asset this fall."

"I promise to make you and everyone else so proud of me."

"We already are, Marilyn," Monica said in her comforting voice. "So are you ready for your speech at the graduation ceremony?"

"I'm ready but nervous too."

"Don't worry you'll do just fine."

"How are you so sure, Mrs. Malone?"

"Marilyn, because you always do."

"Want to hear the first portion of my speech?"

"Yes, I'd be honored but I'll be sure to listen with the same empathy during the ceremony."

"Great it's exciting to hear someone else's opinion besides my parents who have heard it too many times by now."

"Come on let's make our way from this classroom and head outside."

Monica zipped up her leather bag and placed it over her right shoulder. Then the teacher and student walked through the paper riddled halls towards the parking lot. During this time, Monica listened extensively to Marilyn's speech. Once outside, Marilyn continued to the end of her speech. Then Monica gave her a few suggestions and the two prepared to say good-bye.

"Thanks so much on the pointers for my speech," said Marilyn. "I feel even more comfortable now. I'll see you in a couple of days at the graduation."

"Yes, Marilyn, I'll see you then. But in the meantime go have some fun with your classmates."

"Alright Mrs. Malone I guess you're right."

"A little fun isn't going to kill you. I'll see you later."

"Okay," Marilyn said smiling.

Monica made her way to the faculty area of the parking lot while Marilyn went in the opposite direction. Now it was time for her to head to her mother's house and pick up the twins.

As Monica drove down Northside Drive, she decided to give me a call to see how my day was going so far. Keeping her hands on the steering wheel, she used the Bluetooth option in the Tahoe to dial me at work.

"Hi, sweetheart," I said picking up the handset from my desk as I recognized my wife's number.

"Hello, honey. What are you up to?"

"I just finished another round of designs for the revitalization project and now I have to meet with Mr. Bradshaw in an hour."

"I see you're staying busy over there."

"Yeah, but that's a good thing," I said while I took a moment and looked out my window. "So enough about me, how was your last day at school with your students?"

"Happy and also sad too."

"Why do you say that?"

"You know, Aaron, I hate to see them go."

"I know Monica but it's part of the process. Just think about it, you're educating some of our future lawyers, doctors, and even architects."

"I understand but I always get so emotional at this time of the year," she said with a hint of sadness in her voice. "I had one of my smartest students approach me after school today."

"You mean the girl who was elected as class valedictorian you're always talking about?"

"Yes, that's the one."

"Um, what's her name again?"

"It's Marilyn."

"Okay, I remember now. So what happened with her?"

"She just let me know how much I inspired her this year."

"But Monica that's a great statement to hear from one of your students. Maybe you should relay that to your father so he would quit trying to recruit you over to Emory."

"That's so funny, Aaron," she said with a light laugh.

"See, I knew I would cheer you up with that one."

"You always seem to know how to."

"I bet I can guess what is going to cheer you up even more," I said.

"What's that, Aaron?"

"Those bright smiles on the twins face this afternoon."

"You guessed right," she said as I could see her smiling through the phone. "I'm actually turning off Northside Drive now headed to Dunwoody."

"Well, kiss them for me first when you pick them up."

"I will, honey. So what time will you get home tonight?"

"It's hard to say. It probably will be late as usual."

"Well, the boys and I will see you later tonight either way."

"Okay, I'll see you all soon."

Monica continued driving until her Tahoe reached the driveway of her parent's home. Anxiously, she darted inside to see her two boys that meant so much to her. Her mother was the first person she saw as she walked through the front door.

"Monica, there you are," said her mother greeting her. "I thought I heard you pulling up."

"Hi mom," replied Monica. "Yes, it's me."

"So how was your last day at school?"

"Fulfilling as always, mom"

"That's so good to hear, Monica, despite what your father may think."

"So where is dad, anyway?"

"He had another one of his lecturing classes this afternoon over at Emory. Then he said he would be in his office at the university to catch up on a new book he is writing."

"I wonder what his new book is going to be about."

"Only God knows, Monica. He keeps his writing subjects top secret around here until the book has been published and hits the bookstore shelves."

"Yeah, dad has always been odd when it comes to his writing," Monica said to her mother as the women stood near the front door. "So how was your day with the twins?"

"It was grand as always but I'm going to miss my boys since you're now officially on your summer break."

"Don't worry, mom, I'm sure I'll need your help looking after those two. They can keep me quite busy and are a handful."

"Well, cherish the time you spend with them, dear, because one day they will be all grown up. Then you'll be wondering how the time went by so fast."

"For now, I can only imagine that. So where are those two little busy bodies anyway?"

It was as if the two boys waited until the women began to talk about them before they ran wildly into the area where Monica and her mother were. Brandon was leading the way and his brother was a close second.

"Mommy," shouted the two boys together. "You're finally here."

Monica saw the stampede approaching her. She quickly placed both of her knees on the wood floor and extended her arms wide open. The twins, who were running in their white socks, slid perfectly into their mother's heartwarming arms.

"There you two are," Monica said to her sons as she kissed them on their foreheads. "Where have you two been?"

"We were watching the animals on TV," Brandon said.

"Yeah, mommy, and we saw the giant panda like the one at the zoo," Braylon said following up after his older brother.

"Let's get your things together and get ready to go home now so grandma can get some rest."

"Monica, why don't you and the boys stay for dinner?" asked her mother. "I was just about to begin cooking."

"You don't have to go through all that trouble, mom. Besides, I need to stop by the cleaners before they close today."

"Yeah, and I want pizza!" blurted out Brandon still in his mother's arm.

"Can we have pizza tonight?" asked Braylon happy that his brother made the suggestion.

"Maybe but only if you two hurry up and put on your shoes then gather your stuff."

The two boys frantically jumped out of their mother's arms as the thought of being rewarded with pizza excited them. Within sixty seconds flat they had returned with their Velcro strapped shoes on and each carrying a small bag containing a few toys.

"Well, I'll see you later, Monica," her mother said giving her daughter a hug. "Now, you two boys come over here and give your grandma a good-bye kiss."

As she ordered, the twins did just that. Then she held them a little bit extra longer as she hugged them.

"Now, you two behave and enjoy the rest of your evening," she said. "Grandma loves you."

"Good-bye, grandma, we love you too," said the twins together.

Monica led the two out the front door as they waved good-bye to their grandmother. Once they were strapped into their car seats, Monica blew the horn on the Tahoe letting her mother know they were departing.

About five minutes into the drive on the winding back road to Sandy Springs the vehicle accelerated towards the occupant's destination. Monica noticed how quickly she was approaching the red Toyota that was in front of her. She pressed the brake pedal slightly but nothing happened. Before rear ending the vehicle in front of her, she quickly turned the steering wheel into the lane of oncoming traffic noticing that lane was clear. Narrowly, she evaded striking the Toyota and expeditiously turned back into her lane.

"What the hell is going on with this car?" she said in a frantic voice.

"Mommy, you said a bad word," Brandon stated while looking out the window he was seated next to.

"Brandon, be quiet while mommy is driving."

Without alarming the boys, something was terribly wrong, Monica attempted to remain calm. Meanwhile, the vehicle's speed was now up to almost sixty miles per hour and steadily increasing. She took both of her feet and pressed firmly on the brake pedal which went all the way to the floor board. The vehicle didn't stop.

"Mommy, I like it when you go fast," yelled Braylon from the back seat as he noticed cars zipping by in the opposite lane. "Let's go faster!"

"Hey, you just past the pizza place, mommy," Brandon screamed out loud. "Turn around and go back."

Ahead of the vehicle awaited a bigger dilemma. Monica noticed the rear end of a dump truck. On the opposite lane cars were zooming by and she couldn't afford to turn into that lane like last time.

"Hey, slow down you asshole!" shouted out an angry man sticking his head out of his car. He passed the Tahoe on the other side of the road going in the opposite direction. "This is a public street."

"Monica didn't pay any attention to his comment but only noticed her vehicle's speed was now up to seventy miles per hour. The posted speed signs clearly stated forty-five on the slow-moving road. Both of her feet continued to press the brake pedal to no avail. Quickly, she pushed the OnStar emergency button located on the rear-view mirror. She could see the fear that now existed in her sons eyes as the vehicle continued to pick up speed.

"OnStar emergency services," said the friendly woman's voice through the vehicle's system. "Who am I speaking with?"

"This is Monica Malone," she said practically screaming by now.

"Yes, ma'am, I'm showing you as the owner of the vehicle. Is everything okay?"

"No, the brakes on my Tahoe don't work. I'm about to collide with a dump truck in front of me."

"Mrs. Malone please remain calm. I'm going to try and override the braking system on your vehicle."

"Please hurry!"

Monica's heart raced faster as she could hear the woman typing away on her computer. Meanwhile, her Tahoe had now reached a speed of eighty. The twins were beginning to cry as they knew something was wrong.

"Try pressing your brakes now, Mrs. Malone."

"Nothing is happening!"

Monica continued to hear the woman frantically typing as she noticed the vehicle speed was now up to ninety. It was either slam into the vehicle in front of her or turn into oncoming traffic.

"Mommy, we're scared!" yelled the twins from the back.

"Mrs. Malone, please try to press your brakes again," said the OnStar emergency operator.

Monica didn't even have time as she did the only thing that her instincts told her to do. She turned the vehicle off the road thus avoid striking the dump truck or oncoming traffic. The Tahoe's two left wheels rose off the payment causing it to flip multiple times down a ravine. The operator could hear cries and screams from the passengers inside. During the rollover, the Tahoe struck a large oak tree cutting the tree in half. The upper portion of the tree came crashing down on top of the vehicle as it came to a halt.

"Mrs. Malone can you hear me?" asked the friendly operator. "Mrs. Malone are you alright?"

Smoke, dust, and the smell of oil and gas filled the area where the vehicle was now positioned on its side. The front windshield was completely removed from the vehicle. A young man who witnessed the Tahoe leave the road a few seconds ago rushed down the ravine to help.

"She's shaken up pretty bad," shouted the young man to the operator as he stood in front of the dangled mess. Monica let out a faint moan which he barely heard. "Shit and it doesn't look so good for the kids in the back! I'm going to get help."

CHAPTER 17

Today had to be the worst day of my life as I sat next to my wife on the front pew inside New Hope C.M.E. Church in Sandy Springs. Heavy tears continued to flow down her face and onto her black dress as I wrapped my arm around her attempting to comfort her . The handkerchief I had given her earlier was already soaked which served little purpose now. Next to us were Dr. Carmichael and his wife, Allison, who was emotionally distraught as well. Allison's crying and moaning was uncontrollable as her husband did his best to calm her down. Everyone in the church has long faces as the organist, positioned near the pulpit, continued to play the dreaded funeral music while a few more people walked in.

My eyes were glued onto the two white caskets that were in front of me. A colorful arrangement of flowers adorned on top of them. Inside the caskets, lay Brandon and Braylon who had perished in the wreck four days earlier.

Their bodies were so mangled we were compelled to keep the caskets closed instead of the traditional view of an open casket. I still couldn't bring myself to believe my sons were gone and no longer with us. Some psychologist called this 'denial' which is the first stage of grief. Up until the funeral, I still hadn't even shed a tear. I felt guilty for my emotions or lack thereof. Before I could think any further, the soft music faded out, the pastor rose from his chair, and walked up to the podium on the pulpit.

"Today, I stand before you as a man of God," began Pastor McGregor to the church. "And to let you know this is a day of celebration rather than a day of sorrow."

"Oh, I want my beautiful grandchildren back!" yelled out Allison before Pastor McGregor barely finished his sentence. She was crying more frantically now and looked upwards towards the heavens.

"Allison, please try to hold it together," whispered Dr. Carmichael as he held his wife tighter.

Monica turned away from the view in front of us and simply buried her head in my chest while sobbing even more. I tried to console her as best as I could but I knew there was little I could do now.

"For the word says in the book of Philippians for to me, living is Christ and dying is gain," continued Pastor

McGregor. "I am here to let you know that Brandon and Braylon have gone on and gained an eternal life with Christ so rejoice and do not be sad."

"Amen Pastor McGregor," said a woman clapping her hands sitting in a pew a few rows behind us.

Those were the last words I heard from the eulogy as my mind mentally blocked out everything else that was being said. I could only think of all the prior joyous occasions with my sons as the images flooded my mind. Like when the two were born and how I almost fainted in the delivery room. And their first steps I captured with my digital camera recording the entire event. Even more recently, the twins' birthday party which only seemed like seconds ago.

"Aaron, we have to go now," said Monica snapping me out of my trance. "The service is over and we have to join the procession to the cemetery."

"Are you okay, Monica?" I asked as I noticed the service had ended.

"I guess so but I still can't believe our sons are gone, Aaron."

"Don't worry, sweetheart, we are going to get through this. I promise you that."

"But I feel so guilty for what happened. If only I could have done something different."

"Monica, it's not your fault," I said continuing to hold my wife. "We've already discussed that."

Without saying another word Monica buried her face into my chest again and continued to sob more. Then momentarily I helped her to her feet. The Carmichael's stood up slowly next and followed us as we made our way towards the aisle. Once there, a few familiar faces approached us.

"Mrs. Malone, may I extend my deepest condolences and sympathy to you and your family," said the well-dressed man extending his hand to my wife.

The friendly man was no one other than Mr. Bradshaw. He went above and beyond making us feel secure during our time of crisis once he initially heard about the car accident. He even rushed to the hospital and showed unconditional love and support. Surprisingly, he even offered to pay for the entire funeral expenses.

"Thank you again, Mr. Bradshaw," said Monica shaking his hand then she gave him a warm hug. "You've been so supportive all this time."

"You're more than welcome," he said to her then focused his attention to me.

"So how have you been doing, Aaron?" he asked.

"I'm managing, Mr. Bradshaw."

"Well, you just hang on in there. It's all going to work out and get better."

We both hugged as if we were related and I felt a sense of genuine love I thought a man like him could never possess. It was the human and kind side of him I had never seen outside the corporate doors of Donaldson and Bradshaw. When our hug had concluded, Mr. Bradshaw stepped over to the Carmichael's extending kind words of sympathy also.

As soon as Mr. Bradshaw was out of our view up walks my good friend and colleague from work, Sebastian. His eyes were heavy, as if he hadn't been asleep, and a worried look was on his face. Next to him was Tiffany who had a disbelief demeanor about her. At the moment, I couldn't get upset she was at the twins' funeral and this was definitely not the place to let my emotions show, especially in front of my wife.

"Aaron, how have you been holding up?" asked Sebastian as he came into our circle.

"I'm holding on, Sebastian."

"You have to remain strong in these tough times, Aaron. Although, you know I'm here for you if you ever need anything."

After his comment, I simply nodded as if to let him know I already knew that. He was a close friend I had counted on for so many years and it was times like these he was still there for me. Sebastian then quickly turned his attention to Monica.

"Monica, I'm so sorry for your loss," he said with a straight face. "I know the twins meant everything to you."

"Yes, Sebastian, they were everything and much more to Aaron and I," Monica said as her eyes began to fill with tears again. "But we thank you for all the love and support during this tragedy in our lives."

As the pair hugged, I looked directly into the eyes of Tiffany who was still standing nearby. She looked at me as if she didn't know what to say or how to react. Then Sebastian interrupted my stare.

"Hey, you all remember Tiffany from the twins' birthday party," he said looking at her.

"Yes, I think we all became quite familiar with Tiffany at the twins' birthday party," I said in a monotone voice.

"Thank you for coming out for the service, Tiffany," Monica said as she looked towards her.

"Oh, Monica, please don't hesitate to let me know if there is anything I can do for you or Aaron," Tiffany said in a kind and relaxed voice. "I cannot even begin to phantom how you feel right now. I'm so sorry for your loss."

Monica simply gave a hint of a smile at Tiffany's goodwill gesture.

"Well, we better get going, Monica," I said as I stepped closer to her. "I'm sure our limo is all lined up outside and awaits us."

The Carmichael's continued to follow us after they also spoke to Sebastian and Tiffany. Then a few steps into our short stride we encountered a few more people we knew including Jane, Shanna, Marilyn, and plenty of our co-workers. They all were very welcoming and sadden by what had recently happened. Monica had missed Marilyn's speech and the graduation ceremonies but everyone from the school understood. When our brief conversation had ended with all of them, we finally made it inside the limo and were off to the cemetery.

At the gravesite, the mood was more dismal than it was inside the church. Both caskets were hoisted above an empty grave with the unearth dirt nearby. Only a handful of people attended the burial as we only wanted it to be viewed by a selected few.

Pastor McGregor stood in front of the caskets preparing to say a few words as the small crowd gathered around. I noticed two men in the distance dressed in overalls and holding large shovels in their hands. They had taken off their hats in observance of the burial and to give respect for the dead. It was obvious it was their job to shovel the unearth dirt back on top of the caskets once they were retired to the ground below.

"The LORD is my shepherd, I shall not want," said Pastor McGregor firmly as he commenced the recital of Psalm 23. "He maketh me to lie down in green pastures, he leadeth me besides the still waters, he restoreth my soul."

The mechanical pulley system inched the twins' caskets slowly downward into the dark and black grave as Pastor McGregor continued to speak. It was at this point, Monica and I stood and watched as our sons were being buried. It seems as if all the emotions I had been holding in for the last few days came pouring out of me all at once. Tears were running down my face like a raging river and I didn't attempt to wipe them away. Ironically, when I looked at Monica her face was dry and her eyes were tearless. I figured she had shed enough tears and now it was my turn.

"It's all my fault, Aaron," she said maintaining a sober face while continuing to watch the caskets being lowered into the ground. "I should have pulled the emergency brake or shift the vehicle into neutral."

"No, sweetheart, it's not your fault," I said finally wiping away the tears off my face. "You have to stop blaming yourself."

"I can't Aaron. I just can't."

Monica began to cry again as she had done before in the church. I quickly latched onto her and pulled her into my chest.

"It's going to be alright," I said to her in an emotional voice. "The twins are in heaven looking down at us smiling. They're in a better place, Monica, and you have to believe that."

As I continued to hold Monica, I noticed Allison sobbing a bit louder as the caskets had almost reached their destination. Dr. Carmichael was doing his best to hold back his tears but eventually they came down his face.

"Surely goodness and mercy shall follow me all the days of my life," continued Pastor McGregor coming to the end of the verse. "And I will dwell in the house of the LORD forever."

It was as if the mechanical pulley system has a mind of its own because it stopped once Pastor McGregor had finished his last words. I reached down and took a handful of unearth dirt and evenly tossed it on top of Brandon's casket first. Then I repeated the process for Braylon's casket. After which, I took Monica by the hand and led her back to the limo so we could go home.

PART III

A WIFE'S INTUITION

CHAPTER 18

The annoying alarm on my cell phone was going off letting me know it was six o'clock in the morning. I lay in the bed on my back facing the ceiling in a blank stare. Without turning, my hand found the device causing the early-morning ruckus and I turned it off. It had been three days since the funeral and nothing really had changed.

"Sweetheart, are you okay?" I asked Monica who as lying with her back next to me.

"Yes, Aaron, I'm fine."

"How did you sleep last night?"

"Not well at all."

"Maybe you should think about taking those pills your doctor prescribed to help you sleep."

"You mean those Ambien pills?"

"Yes."

"No, Aaron, I'm not putting that medication into my body."

"But you have to try to get some decent sleep sooner or later."

"Well, I guess it will have to be later."

Monica finally turned over on her side where she was facing me and placed her arm on my chest. Then she began to slowly rub on my chest while looking at me.

"Do you love me, Aaron?" she asked.

"Yes," I said a little confused while turning my head away from the ceiling to look at her. "Why do you ask?"

"I just wanted to. There's no rhyme or reason."

"I had better get up and start my day," I said turning my head while looking up at the ceiling once more. "I can stay here with you again today if you want me to."

"No, honey, you better go to work today. I'll be alright."

"Are you sure?"

"Yes, my mother is coming by later to check on me."

"Well, that's good. Maybe you two can go out and do something together."

"Yeah, that's what she suggested too."

Monica then shifted her body away from me and moved out of the bed. She grabbed her robe which rested near the foot of the bed and slowly placed it on.

"So where are you going?" I asked turning towards her again.

"Downstairs to make some breakfast for you," she replied with her back towards me.

"Monica, don't worry about that. I can pick up something quick to eat on my way into the office."

"Okay, Aaron, but I'm going to put on a hot pot of coffee," she said turning around to face me and closing up her robe. "Do you want some?"

"Sure, I'll take some."

My wife disappeared downstairs and my feet found my slippers which were next to the bed. While standing up, I yawned and stretched as the mental anguish over the last few days were finally catching up to me. I slowly walked over to one of the bedroom windows and peeked out the wooden blinds. The streetlights were still on as the sun was beginning to come up. I let out another yawn and then headed to the bathroom for my customary shave and shower.

After forty-five minutes in the bathroom and another fifteen minutes getting dressed, I headed downstairs. Before I did, I passed the twins' room which hadn't been touched since their departure. Their twin beds were perfectly made, and even their new soccer ball remained all alone in the middle of the room. I soaked in all the cherished memories for a few more moments then moved on.

In the kitchen, Monica sat at the table sipping on her coffee out of a China cup. Absent was the familiar noise that Brandon and Braylon were known for during this time of the morning. Beside her, were an empty chair and a cup of coffee with steam brewing from it. I took my seat there.

"How did you know I was coming downstairs?" I asked looking at the coffee cup in front of me.

"It's called a wife's intuition," she said after taking another sip of coffee. "Besides, I heard you coming anyway."

"This coffee is perfect, sweetheart," I said after I took a sip from my cup. "Two teaspoons of sugar and a hint of cream just the way I like it."

"You sure you don't want some sunny-side-up eggs and a few slices of bacon?"

"No, it's almost seven-thirty and I need to get going," I said then took another sip from my cup. "So are you sure you're going to be alright?"

"Yes. My mother called while you were upstairs and she should be over here in about an hour."

"Okay, but I'll periodically call you throughout the day while I'm at work."

I took one final sip from my cup and stood up. Then I leaned over and kissed my wife good-bye.

"I love you, Monica," I said with a smile.

"I love you too, Aaron," she replied back.

Driving out the community, I saw Mr. Newman with Jewels like so many times before. I simply blew my horn and gave a friendly wave. As always, Jewels barked and Mr. Newman smiled and waved back.

I decided to take the scenic route to work and traveled down Roswell Road. After driving for a few miles, I decided to make an adjustment in my commute to work. Then I picked up my cell phone and called my secretary, Jane.

"Donaldson and Bradshaw this is Jane speaking," said the always friendly voice on the other end.

"Good morning, Jane, this is Aaron."

"Morning, Mr. Malone, it's not too often you call before you come into work."

"Yeah, I know. I'm just letting you know I'll be in about an hour late."

"Is everything okay, Mr. Malone?"

"Yes, I just have to take care of some early-morning business."

"So how is Mrs. Malone doing?" she asked.

"She is doing better but it just takes time."

"I can imagine, Mr. Malone. Well, my heart and prayers will continue to go out to the both of you."

"Thanks so much, Jane. I'll see you in little bit."

"Okay, I'll see you when you get here."

After I hung up with Jane, I pressed down on the car's accelerator. Unlike the interstate traffic, Roswell Road was moving pretty smoothly. I didn't know where I was going but needed to clear my head and sometimes driving for me was the best antidote.

Roswell Road eventually merged into Peachtree Road as I had now made it to the Buckhead district of Atlanta. I noticed the morning traffic was picking up among the early commuters as I traveled south. There was a landmark that was very familiar to me as I continued my drive. It was St. Vincent Catholic Church and well known to many people. It was the sanctuary I frequent every Sunday with my foster family with whom I lived with during my last two years of high school. Rapidly, I made a u-turn in the middle of Peachtree Road and headed back towards the church. Once there, I parked in the almost empty parking lot and decided to walk into the church.

Inside the tranquil view brought back so many memories from the past. It was like I had stepped back into time and nothing had changed with the church. The enormous colored pastel windows were still there along with the rows of red colored padded pews that never seemed to be worn out. I walked forward on the red carpet that was throughout the church and noticed the same picture of the Virgin Mary and also a picture of the crucifix of Jesus. Then I continued until I entered one of the confessionals.

The confessional was cozy yet spacious enough. I realized I hadn't sat inside one of these in years and felt a sense of guilt about it. After going off to college, it seemed like church was never a priority anymore. A door opened and closed as it was the priest taking a seat in the compartment next to me. There was a small grid that allowed us to speak to one another.

"Bless me Father, for I have sinned," I said softly somewhat ashamed of my actions I was about to admit to.

"Yes, my son," said the familiar voice. "What seems to be your transgression?"

I gathered my thoughts before I answered trying to put a name with the familiar voice I had heard so many times before. Then it was as if a light bulb came on and I realized the priest was Father Flanagan. After all these years, he still presided at the church.

"I'm ashamed to say I have broken one of the Ten Commandments, Father."

"Which one have you broken, my son?"

I took a moment and paused still not sure whether or not to answer. It was awkward for me to tell the priest what I had done.

"I've committed adultery, Father."

"And now you're here to repent, my son?"

"Yes Father."

"Do you actually know what it means to repent?" he asked.

"I believe to ask for forgiveness, Father."

"My son to repent is not a penance for guilt or a quick prayer for forgiveness. Repentance is a complete change of heart which you must utilize in your walk throughout life."

"I see, Father."

"What else seems to be troubling you my son?" asked Father Flanagan. "I sense a heavy burden in your voice."

"My wife and I have recently lost our four-year-old twin boys in a car accident."

"I'm sorry to hear that from you, my son."

"I want to know is this the Lord punishing me for my sin?"

"Our father in heaven, Jesus Christ, does not send harm my son. He may allow a crisis in your life as a test of your faith to him and to capture your attention."

"Yes, Father, but I am having trouble comprehending the death of my sons."

"One must not question our father in heaven as he knows what is right. Let yourself be healed in Christ and progress in the life of the Spirit. Go in peace, my son, as I will continue to pray for you and your wife."

"Thank you, Father."

I wiped a few tears that had flowed down my cheeks before I exited the confessional. I guess speaking with Father Flanagan was the release I so desperately needed that had built up inside of me. When I reached the inside of my car, I noticed it was barely past nine o'clock.

The mood in the office was still about business when I walked through the large glass doors at Donaldson and Bradshaw. I straighten my tie as I could see Jane's desk in the near distance. When I reached her, she stopped me before I could utter a single word out.

"Mr. Malone, its perfect timing to see you," she said placing the phone from her ear back on the receiver.

"Why do you say that, Jane?"

"That was actually Mr. Bradshaw's secretary calling for you. Mr. Bradshaw would like to see you in his office right away."

"Well, you are right Jane. It seems as if my arrival is perfect timing."

"Would you like for me to call his secretary back and let her know you have arrived?"

"No need for that, Jane. I can just make my way down to Mr. Bradshaw's office now."

I kept a straight face as I turned in the direction of Mr. Bradshaw's office. I didn't want Jane to get any hint of confusion I was actually experiencing now. As I walked briskly, I knew the revitalization project was still on track and all the previous deadlines had been met. So I was a little anxious to know what the boss could want with me now.

"I'm here to see Mr. Bradshaw," I said to his secretary as I walked up to her desk.

"Yes, Mr. Malone, he is expecting you," she said. "Please go ahead right on in."

She motioned for me to enter and presented a sweet smile as always. Then I proceeded forward through the large doors into his office. When I saw him, he was standing behind his desk talking and gesturing with his hands. He was dressed in one of his tailored suits as usual. His audience included Mr. Black and surprisingly, Sebastian.

"Aaron, please come right on in and join us," said Mr. Bradshaw stopping his conversation once he noticed me. "Your secretary informed me you would be running a little late into the office this morning. Is everything okay?"

"Yes, sir, everything is fine," I said as I moved closer and finally stopped in front of his desk. "I just had to take care of some unfinished business I had been avoiding for a while."

"Very well, Aaron," he said with a concerned look on his face. "As you can see we are joined by Mr. Black and Sebastian."

"Yes, I see," I said turning to both of them. "Good morning, gentlemen."

"Good morning, Aaron," said Sebastian eagerly.

Mr. Black, on the other hand, remained silent as always and simply nodded in response. I noticed he had his patented mini briefcase by his side.

"Well, Aaron, please take a seat," suggested Mr. Bradshaw while he continued to stand.

I took a seat in front of his desk wondering what this meeting was all about. Next to me sat Sebastian and Mr. Black who looked on.

"Aaron, I know you've been going through some emotional and tough personal setbacks within the last few days," began Mr. Bradshaw into his short speech. "And I know it can be very challenging as well. Therefore, in order to help alleviate any stress you may have encountered, I decided to reassign the revitalization project to Sebastian."

"What?" I said looking a bit confused and shocked.

"It's only a temporary assignment, Aaron," said Mr. Bradshaw. "I'm also going to suggest you take a few weeks off, with pay of course, from work."

"In all due respect, Mr. Bradshaw, I feel I'm fully capable of handling the revitalization project solely by myself as before. And I rather not take any time off."

"Well, Aaron, I admire your commitment and generous loyalty to the firm but my determination is based solely as a business decision."

"Sir, never in all my years here has my work fluctuated on any project assigned to me."

"I am aware of that, Aaron," continued Mr. Bradshaw. "But never in all your years working for Donaldson and Bradshaw had you to deal with a personal situation like you're going through now. Believe me, Aaron, this is a decision based on the firm's best interest. We just have too much at stake to be compromised."

"Yeah, Aaron, it's just on a temporary basis," reiterated Sebastian from his chair. "It's still your project and I'm here to act as a resource for you."

"I feel Sebastian is well qualified to keep the project moving forward," said Mr. Bradshaw. "Like you, he's a senior designer with years of experience. Although he hasn't had the major projects you had in the past, I feel he's quite qualified to keep the revitalization project afloat on an interim basis."

There was no need to try to fight against what Mr. Bradshaw has already made up in his mind. Maybe some time off would help me clear my mind and couldn't hurt me. And besides, the extra time off from work would help me comfort Monica.

"I guess you're right, Mr. Bradshaw," I said slightly disappointed but tried not to let it show. "The extra time off is probably the remedy I need."

"Well, I'm glad you see it the firm's way," said Mr. Bradshaw with a smile. "Now, if you could just transfer all the electronic files over to Sebastian today that would be great. And don't forget to have any and all paper drafts copied to him, too."

"Yes, sir, I'll get on that task right away."

Mr. Bradshaw then finally moved from beyond the back of his desk and towards me. As he walked to me he extended his hand out.

"Thank you for understanding everything, Aaron."

"You're more than welcome, sir," I said as I firmly shook his hand.

Sebastian and Mr. Black had now risen to their feet. We all shook hands with the agreement that had just taken place. Then I made my way back to my office.

"There you are Mr. Malone," said Jane as I came into her view in front of her desk. "Ms. Tiffany Towns has called you three times since you have been in your meeting with Mr. Bradshaw. She said it was urgent she speak with you."

"Well, the next time she calls tell her I'm out of the office and simply send her to my voicemail," I said in a direct tone.

"Yes sir."

"There's one more thing I need for you to complete as soon as possible, Jane."

"Yes, Mr. Malone."

"Pull the complete electronic file for the revitalization project along with all the paper drafts and forward same to Sebastian Carter today."

"Sure thing Mr. Malone," said Jane looking confused.

After my last request to Jane, I retired to my office for some peace of mind. Reclined in my chair from behind my desk, I watched the slow-moving traffic on the interstate attempting to soak in what had just happened.

CHAPTER 19

It was the middle of the evening rush hour and traffic was hectic as usual. Sebastian had just left the office as his brand new fire-red Chevy Camaro inched through downtown Atlanta. Confident with what had transpired earlier in the day he picked up his cell phone and made a call.

"Hello," said the mysterious woman who was his date a few weeks earlier.

"Baby, you're not going to believe what happened to me today," he said in an excited voice.

"Sebastian, is everything alright?"

"It's more than alright, it's great!"

"Well, don't leave me in limbo, what happened?"

"Mr. Bradshaw, my boss, just reassigned the revitalization project to me today. Isn't that great news?"

"Yes, that is," she said with little effort in her voice.

"What's the matter, baby? You don't sound like you're proud of me and my accomplishment."

"I am, Sebastian. It's just I'm somewhat saddened with all that has happened to Aaron."

"Well, don't be. He's strong and will bounce back from it all."

"Yeah, I guess you're right."

"Besides, Mr. Bradshaw only reassigned the revitalization project to me on a temporary basis. However, it's just enough time for me to show and prove to him how talented I am."

"So maybe that promotion you have been seeking is actually right around the corner."

"Absolutely," he said more confident than ever. "Now, it's time for us to celebrate."

"How did I already know you were going to say that?" she asked with a smile.

"Because we're made for each other," he answered. "Listen, I'm actually in your vicinity and wanted to come by with a bottle of champagne."

"That's fine, Sebastian, I would love for you to do that. I'm in bed right now with something real sexy on."

"Well, you just stay put because I'll be there shortly."

Light rain began to fall as the two disconnected their call. Sebastian quickly turned on his windshield wipers along with his headlights. He knew he'd better get to his destination fast as traffic would go from hectic to horrible once the rain drops increased.

"Now, where can I find a liquor store around here?" he asked himself exiting off the Seventeenth Street Bridge.

Then like a mirage that would appear to a lost survivor in the desert, he focused his eyes on bright neon lights ahead of him. The sign clearly read: The Liquor Store.

"How fitting," he said out loud as he maneuvered his car closer to the store in front of him. "That's what I call keeping it simple."

He finally stopped his car in front of the tiny establishment while he noticed the parking lot is full. Then he finds a parking spot on the street nearby. After he exits his vehicle, he jogs to the front door of the liquor store as the rain drops were falling faster now. As he enters the store, a bell chimes and he notices a man who looks to be of Arab descent standing behind the counter.

"Where's your champagne?" Sebastian barked out.

"Towards the back near the beer cooler, sir," answered the friendly man pointing.

Sebastian made his way back to where the man had instructed him to go. As he did, he heard the door bell chimed again behind him as another patron had entered the store. While standing in front of the champagne bottle display, he contemplated which brand to select. Finally, he grabbed one bottle of Moet, hesitated for a moment, and picked up a second bottle.

"Well, aren't we celebrating really big tonight," said a woman who walked up to the wine display next to where he was standing.

Sebastian actually got a whiff of her seductive perfume before she started speaking. The scent was light yet strong enough to peak his attention and interest. When he turned to her, he noticed the attractive woman wearing a black cocktail dress. Her figure was impressive too.

"Oh, it's just a little joyous celebration for tonight," he said. "Nothing too major I can't handle."

"Well, maybe you can help me out in selecting a good wine."

"Sure, what's the occasion?" he asked admiring her as she turned her attention back to the platform of wine in front of her.

"My date and I are going to a friend's independent film screening tonight."

"Wow, that sounds like some real fun."

"Yeah, I just wanted to unwind the night down afterwards with a little bit of wine," she said still looking indecisive. "But I can't decide on whether to go with a red or white wine."

"Red wines are mostly served while dining out and can be a bit heavy. White wines are more commonly sipped for relaxation."

"I knew a sophisticated man like you would have the right answer," she said. "So, I should get the white wine, right?"

"That would be an excellent choice," he said smiling back at her as she picked up a bottle of white wine. "The register is this way, as always, ladies first."

As Sebastian motioned for the woman to move ahead of him, his eyes were glued to her backside as she walked. When they arrived at the counter, there were two customers ahead of them.

Then out of the blue and unexpectedly, a man opens the front door into the liquor store. The doorbell chimes again as he remains outside, yet holds the door open, looking in.

"Darlene, what the heck is taking you so long?" he angrily screams out as he's dressed in a black tuxedo. "I thought you said it would only take you two minutes to pick out some wine."

"I'm coming, Bradley," she snapped back at him. "Can't you see I'm at the register, now?"

The man looked at her in disgust and then eyeballs Sebastian. Finally, he closes the front door of the liquor store and heads back to his car.

"He can be so damn impatient sometimes," she said looking a little embarrassed at the commotion her date caused. "I'll be glad when the night is over."

Sebastian took this opportunity to pull his business card from his pocket and presented it to the woman.

"Well, if you're looking for less stress and no drama maybe we can meet for lunch sometimes," he said handing her his card. "By the way, I'm Sebastian."

"Yes, I think I would like that," she said grabbing the card then placing it in her tiny purse. "It's nice to meet you, Sebastian."

"Ma'am, are you ready to check out?" asked the man from behind the counter.

"Oh, I'm sorry," she said turning her attention away from Sebastian. "Is it my turn already?"

"Yes ma'am," replied the man politely.

She took a few steps closer and placed the bottle of wine on the counter as Sebastian followed closely behind her. The man quickly scanned the wine through the point-of-sale system and began to place her wine in a bag.

"Is that all for you, ma'am?" the man asked.

"Yes, that's it," she replied back.

"Actually, you can add these two bottles of Moet and I'll pay for everything," Sebastian quickly said placing his items on the counter.

"Sebastian, you don't have to go through all the trouble and pay for my bottle of wine," she said with an astonished look.

"It's no problem at all, Darlene," Sebastian said with a simple grin.

A few more customers began to mount up behind Sebastian as the man behind the counter now scanned the two bottles of champagne through the register. Then he handed Darlene her bottle of wine.

"Well, I'll see you later, Sebastian, and thanks again for everything," she said with a glow.

"Yes, I will and you're very welcome," was Sebastian simple response.

She took her bottle of wine and walked out the liquor store. Sebastian kept his eyes on her backside again continuing to smile.

"Will that be debit or credit, sir?" asked the man interrupting Sebastian's thoughts.

"Always credit," he said handing the man his American Express card but kept his eyes firmly on the woman he had just met until she was out of his view.

By the time Sebastian reached his car, the rain was coming down in buckets. Agitated slightly, because he had gotten wet, he quickly opened his drivers' side door and dove inside the confines of his car. The two bottles of Moet rested in the passenger side seat next to him.

"Now, that's what I like to hear," he said to himself as the rain bounced off his Camaro's roof. "That's good music to have sex to."

He turned on the car by pressing the start button which was located near the steering wheel. Then he pressed the gas pedal until the engine revved up making a loud howling noise. The double dual exhaust blew out a colorless smoke from the car's rear end. A split second after putting the car in drive he punched the accelerator onto his final destination.

As the wide high-performance tires parted the water on the roads and hugged the black pavement, Sebastian continued to go faster. With the engine growling even louder, he felt his muscle car was superior to any vehicle on the street and he had the horsepower to prove it. Driving dangerously fast through downtown, with his adrenaline rushing, he finally turned with precision into the high-rise condo's parking garage which was dry and well lit. Once he found a parking space he took a moment and continued to listen as the Camaro's engine purred like a kitten not missing a beat.

"Damn, I love this car!" he exclaimed out. "It's the power and style I've been searching for.

Then he calmly turned off his toy and grabbed the two bottles of champagne. The woman upstairs was patiently waiting for him to arrive and he didn't want to disappoint her.

Sebastian managed to find the woman's residence quite easy this time without getting confused. Once he reached the front door, he lightly knocked and waited for a response. He heard someone walking to the door from the inside and then saw a familiar face as the door opened.

"There you finally are," said the woman standing on the on the other side of the door. "I was beginning to worry about you since it's raining so hard outside."

"There's nothing my new Camaro can't handle," he said making his way into her residence. "Not even a little rain."

"The woman closed the door behind him. She was dressed in one of his white tee shirts which hardly covered her purple laced panties.

"Well, you look sexy barely dressed," he said clutching the champagne bottles close to his chest.

"I thought you would like it," she said. "It's simple and straight to the point."

The two finally embraced after their short dialogue had ended. He kissed her to let her know he missed her.

"Come on, let's go to your bedroom," he said after their kiss had concluded.

"Wait a minute, Sebastian, you're always so anxious."

"Good news and what I'm looking at now makes me so horny."

"Well, let's make a toast and celebrate the good news first," she said stepping back from him. "What's in the bag?"

"A few bottles of Moet," he answered.

"Okay, then follow me into the kitchen so I can get the glasses."

Sebastian did as he was instructed and walked behind the sexy woman as his imagination began to unravel. His eyes were looking through her tee shirt as if he had x-ray vision.

Once the pair reached the kitchen, she reached into the cherry-stained cabinet, with her back towards him, looking for the perfect glasses. Sebastian impatiently pulled out one of the bottles of champagne from the bag and began to open it. He managed to pop the bottle open, keeping it in his hand, as fizz and suds from the champagne flowed down the bottle. It would eventually find its way to the hard-wood floors he was standing on. Then he took the entire bottle and turned it up cowboy style.

"Sebastian, what are you doing?" she asked turning around after she found the glasses. "You're making a mess all over the kitchen floor."

He failed to answer her question and simply moved closer to her. Suddenly, he violently grabbed the back of her long hair.

"Come over here and kiss me again," he said in a demanding tone.

"Sebastian, stop it you're hurting me!"

"I thought you like the aggressive side of me."

"I do but this is ridiculous," she said sounding frightened and barely holding on to the two glasses.

He kissed her again but this time much longer than when he first walked through the door. After that, he placed the bottles of champagne on the counter. Then in a quick fashion, he takes his huge hands and rips her tee shirt completely off. The glasses she was once carrying fall to the hard-wood floor and shatters instantly. Shocked, surprised, and scared by his actions she looks into his menacing eyes while standing there in her panties.

"Now, take my hand and let's go to your bedroom like I requested before," he said in a smooth tone reaching towards her.

She complied with his wishes not wanting to upset him anymore. The two spent the rest of the night in her bedroom as the heavy rain continued to fall.

CHAPTER 20

It was a few minutes after nine o'clock in the morning and I was already bored out of my mind. I didn't know how I planned to spend the next few weeks away from work wondering if the revitalization project was okay in Sebastian's hands. I figured he could handle it although I would give him a courtesy call later in the day just to see how things were going.

Monica was already in the kitchen as I could smell her cooking a light breakfast for us as usual. Apparently, she woke up before I did and managed to take a quick shower before she went downstairs. I noticed our bathroom was still full of steam from her prior use of it as I made my way out of the bed. Quickly, I took a hot shower to rejuvenate my bones then put on some casual clothes and went downstairs.

When I arrived in the kitchen, my plate and cup of coffee were the only items on the table. The plate contained scrambled eggs with melted cheddar cheese, sausage links, and French toast. Monica was just finishing up with the dishes and tiding up the kitchen.

"Well, you seem to be in a better mood this morning," I said to my wife as I walked over to give her a kiss.

"Yes, I feel a little better today, Aaron," she said sounding optimistic. "Spending the day with my mother yesterday helped cheer me up a little."

I noticed Monica was dressed in a pink and white jogging suit and she already had a pair of her Nike running shoes on. Coincidentally, her hair was pulled back in ponytail and she had no make-up on.

"Monica, where are you off to so early this morning?" I asked.

"Oh, Shanna and I decided to meet for an early morning jog," she replied. "It's a good stress reliever and keeps you fit."

"Where do you two plan to go jogging?"

"Piedmont Park because it's safe."

"I can come if you like," I said trying to sound enthusiastic. "It will only take me a few minutes to change into my workout gear."

"No, honey, you can stay put," she said pulling out a chair from the table. "Besides, I don't want your breakfast to get cold. Just take a seat now and enjoy it."

"Yeah, it does look tasty."

I sat in the chair Monica had pulled out for me and then made myself comfortable. After taking a sip of the perfectly brewed coffee, I dug into my breakfast which was still warm.

"Well, I'll see you in a little bit, honey," she said grabbing the keys to the rental car from the kitchen counter.

"Sure thing, sweetheart," I said before stuffing my mouth with scrambled eggs. I chewed and swallowed before I spoke again. "Don't hesitate to call me if you need anything."

"Will do, Aaron."

"Hey, aren't you forgetting something?" I asked while Monica made her way to the front door.

"No, I don't think so," she said halting in her tracks.

"It's your purse, Monica," I pointed out. "You left it on the kitchen counter."

"I don't need my purse to go jogging, silly," she said with laughter. "I'll see you later."

Monica exited the house as I continued to stuff my mouth. By the time she was pulling out the driveway, I was halfway done with my breakfast. The French toast was delicious as I took one bite and it was almost gone. As I prepared to finish the remaining portion off, the house phone located near the kitchen sink rang. I took a quick sip of coffee, wiped my mouth, and made my way out of the chair.

"Malone residence," I said answering the phone somewhat upset the caller had disturbed my breakfast.

"Yes, sir, I'm trying to reach Aaron or Monica Malone," said the female voice on the other end.

"This is Aaron Malone you're speaking to."

"Ah, Mr. Malone, I finally was able to reach you. This is Brenda with Paramount Insurance we insure your automobiles."

"Yes, Brenda, I've already received your settlement check for the total loss damages to the Tahoe," I said in a hurry looking at my plate that I wanted to get back to.

"Actually, sir, I'm calling you on another matter concerning the damaged Tahoe."

"Well, what could that be?"

"Our investigation team found some disturbing evidence with your on-board computer we retrieved from the vehicle," she said. "It's sort of like a black box that are used to record data on airplanes."

"Yeah, I understand that," I said listening more closely to the caller.

"Apparently, we discovered your vehicle's system had been hacked into which caused the brakes to fail."

"Brenda, that sounds too unrealistic to believe," I said scratching my head.

"In reality it's not, Mr. Malone. You see someone with a minicomputer or even a smart phone with the right software could have compromised your vehicle's system with direct access to it."

"Uh-huh, I'm listening."

"But the person or persons responsible for this weren't an average Joe."

"What do you mean by that, Brenda?"

"Sir, I mean it takes a sophisticated mind to be able to reprogram or even crack your vehicle's computer. We believe someone quite familiar with computers or even with an engineering background."

"That sounds very interesting, Brenda," I said. "Tell me more."

"First, let me ask you a simple question, Mr. Malone."

"Sure, go right ahead."

"Did you have your vehicle serviced by someone prior to the accident?"

"No, the last time I had my vehicle serviced was six months ago at the dealership. That was for a routine oil change."

"We estimated that whoever tampered with your vehicle had to do so within a week or two prior to the accident," she said in a confident way. "Do you recall anyone having access to your vehicle during that time frame?"

"Not that I can…"

Before I could finish my sentence my mouth froze with an eerie chill that came over me. I stood in the kitchen looking stunned with my jaw wide open. There was dead silence in the room.

"Mr. Malone, are you still there?" Brenda asked as she listened to the silence.

"No, say it's not so," I finally yelled out shaking my head.

"Sir, are you okay?"

"Brenda, I just realized something and I have to go now."

"But, Mr. Malone, I need your cooperation in order for us to complete our investigation."

"I'll have to call you back later, Brenda," I said angrily and slammed down the phone.

My blood pressure was at a boiling point as I managed to fit the pieces of the puzzle together. There was only one person who had access to the Tahoe, prior to the accident, besides Monica and I. Seems like Tiffany was the culprit, who was in the garage with me, during the twins' birthday party.

I gathered my thoughts and took a deep breath of air. Then I repeated the process again so I could think straight. I still didn't want to believe what my mind was telling me. I fumbled for my car keys which were in my pants and decided it was time to leave.

"Well, it looks like I'm about to pay Ms. Tiffany Towns an unannounced visit at her company's satellite office downtown," I said to myself. "She's been dying to speak to me lately and it's about time we got reacquainted."

Like a madman on a mission I ran to the front door, with keys in hand, anxious to get to my car. As I opened the front door, I was surprised to see who was standing there.

"Good heavens, Aaron, it looks as if you've seen a ghost!"

"Mrs. Chastain, what are you doing here?"

"I was just about to ring your doorbell when you unexpectedly opened the door," she answered still startled.

"Yes, Mrs. Chastain, I was actually on my way out to take care of an urgent matter this morning," I said stepping out of the house and closing the door behind me. "You'll have to excuse me."

"Well, is everything alright, Aaron?" she asked with a concerned look on her face.

"Yes, everything is fine."

"The reason I asked is because you look quite upset."

"Mrs. Chastain, I'm not trying to be obtuse with you but I really must go now," I said walking quickly to my Audi that was parked in the driveway. "We will have to talk later."

"But wait, Aaron, that's not what I came over here for this morning," she said following behind me. "I just wanted to give Monica this cover sleeve for the DVD."

Confused and annoyed by the conversation I was having with Mrs. Chastain, I stopped at my car and turned around to face her. By now, she had made it over to my car as well and was waving the DVD cover sleeve in her hand.

"Monica is gone right now, Mrs. Chastain. However, I'm sure she won't damage the movie you let her watch."

"It wasn't a movie, dear."

"Well, what could be so important that you needed to bring over a DVD cover sleeve to her?"

"You mean she didn't tell you about yesterday evening?"

"No, what on God's green earth happened?"

"Well, I decided to watch what my newly installed surveillance cameras had been recording lately," she said slowly. "And that's when I found something that piqued my interest. Then I called Monica over to take a look with me."

"So what did you see?" I asked with a bit of curiosity.

"I went back and watched the footage from the first day the cameras were installed. It so happened to be the day of the twins' birthday party."

"Yes, I remember that."

"Do you remember the pretty woman your wife introduced me to during the birthday party?"

"Vaguely, but which one are you referring to?"

"She was wearing a pretty pink pastel-colored dress."

"Yes, her name is Tiffany."

"That's the name your wife called out yesterday," she said in agreement. "I can't believe I already forgot her name so quickly. My memory is not what is use to be, Aaron."

"Mrs. Chastain please continue on with the story," I said wanting her to get to the point. "What happened next?"

"Well, that same woman was outside your garage near the side of your house talking to someone on her cell phone," she continued. "It just happened that one of my security cameras caught everything she was saying."

"What was she talking about?"

"Apparently, she was letting the person know on the phone that your wife's Tahoe had been infiltrated and everything was going according to plan," she said looking sad. "And as you know, Aaron, shortly after the twins' birthday party your wife had that terrible accident."

My mind took another blow but what Mrs. Chastain was telling me solidified what Brenda had said earlier.

"Yes, I finally see your point."

"So did your wife, yesterday, after watching what happened. She bolted out of my house but first insisted I let her hold onto the DVD which had the recorded incident."

"Thanks for all your help, Mrs. Chastain," I said opening the door to my car. "But I really must get a move on. And don't worry I think Monica won't let that DVD get damaged. It's a valuable piece of evidence right now."

To make her feel better, I took the DVD cover sleeve out of her hand and tossed it into my car. After I sat down in my car, she spoke again.

"Aaron, it seems like Monica didn't tell you anything about what she and I witnessed yesterday," Mrs. Chastain said.

"That's right she didn't say a word to me," I said finally closing the door to my car. Then I sped out the driveway of my home.

I raced through the downtown connector tying to make it to Marietta Street before my wife did. I knew all hell would break loose if Monica reached the offices of Topaz Consulting Group before I could. But Monica being a savvy person was already two steps ahead of me. She had traveled to Tiffany's condo at the Twelve Hotel at Atlantic Station.

Tiffany didn't go into the office this morning due to a brunch meeting she had with a potential client of hers. She had just slipped on her business dress and was putting on one of her conservative diamond earrings when her doorbell rang. She thought it probably was housekeeping and failed to look through the peephole or ask who it was before opening the door. When she did, it was Monica standing there with a cold stare.

"Monica, what a pleasant surprise to see you again," she said lying through her pearl white teeth. "How did you know where I lived?"

"It's called a wife's intuition," Monica said boldly.

CHAPTER 21

I must have broken a dozen traffic laws and almost caused a major accident trying to get to Tiffany's office. I was finally on Marietta Street and could see her office in my sight. Without time to spare, I pulled my car into a no parking spot right in front of the one-story office building. The last thing on my mind was trying to find an available parking space in busy downtown Atlanta.

As I entered the quaint office, a receptionist was sitting behind a desk and perked up immediately. Behind her were several rows of low portioned cubicles where many employees were busy working. The majority of them turned their attention to the front entrance where I stood.

"I need to see Tiffany Towns right now," I demanded looking straight into the receptionist's blue eyes.

"May I ask what it is in regards to, sir?" she asked so eloquently.

"It's rather personal to be quite honest with you," I said getting to the point. "But if you must know she worked as a consultant for my firm, Donaldson and Bradshaw, on the revitalization project at the old General Motors assembly plant."

The receptionist began typing fast on the keyboard to her computer which was in front of her. Soon, she finally found the information she was looking for and spoke out before I could.

"Yes, sir, I'm showing her consulting services have already ended with your firm."

"So, where the hell is she?" I asked angrily.

"I'm sorry we can't divulge any information on our employees, sir."

"Well, it looks like I'm going to have to find her myself."

All eyes were really fixed on me now in the front as my voice resonated back to the cubicles. The employees had a concerned look on their face not knowing what to expect next. I took it upon myself to walk past the receptionist's desk and into the rows of cubicles.

"Sir, you can't go back there," she said standing up out of her chair. "That's a restricted area for employees only."

"Well, not at this moment," I said walking slowly and looking for Tiffany's pretty face.

The receptionist sat back down, picked up the phone, and began to dial a number. While doing this, she continued to keep her eyes on me.

"Where the hell are you, Tiffany!" I screamed out as I walked at a snail's pace. "You have some serious explaining to do."

"Oh my God," said a frightened woman placing her hand over her chest as I walked up to her cubicle. "I hope you're not going to do something crazy, I have two young kids at home."

I shook my head at her as she wasn't the scumbag I was looking for. Then I continued my journey as everyone remained completely silent.

"Come on, Tiffany, don't be so bashful now," I screamed louder as I looked around the area I was in. "It's Jack and I promise you I won't be a dull boy today."

As I pass another row of cubicles, I came across two women huddled up together. There was an obvious look of fear in their eyes as I glanced at them for a second. Then I moved on.

"I swear that man has lost his freaking mind," said one of the two women after I was no longer in their view.

"Be quiet, Irene, before he hears you," her friend said back to her.

After the small disturbance I had caused, a man began to approach me. He was wearing a suit and seemed to be rather upset.

"Sir, I'm the operations manager," he said with an attitude. "We run a respectable and reputable business here. And we don't condone someone coming in here ranting and raving as you have."

"Listen, buster," I said putting my index finger in his face. "You better get Tiffany out here now or it's going to get worse."

He quickly moved backwards as I saw a sense of intimidation in his eyes. He knew I meant business and really didn't care at what expense.

"Melissa, call the police," he yelled out to the receptionist who was still looking on from the front entrance.

Meanwhile, I looked around disappointed and realized Tiffany wasn't in the small office. Even so, I did know where to look next and that was her condo at Atlantic Station.

"Well, when they get here, tell them to meet me at Tiffany's condo at the Twelve Hotel," I said moving fast back to the front door. "It's on the twenty-fifth floor."

I ran past the receptionist who was busy on the phone calling the police and bolted out the front door. Outside, I picked my way through the mass of pedestrians walking on the sidewalk. When I made it to my car, there was a meter maid standing there writing me a ticket.

"Hey, I was only parked there for a second," I said looking shocked.

"A no parking zone means just that, sir," she said placing the ticket on my windshield.

"Come on, ma'am, cut me some slack," I said with empathy. "I swear it was an emergency I had to tend to."

"Tell it to the judge," she said as if my concerns didn't bother her one bit. Then she blended in with the rest of the pedestrians on the sidewalk moving away.

I snatched the nominal parking ticket off my windshield and jumped into my car. I decided to travel the surface streets until I made it to the Twelve Hotel. When I did, there was no time to find a parking space. So I simply pulled up to valet parking, left my car running, and jumped out. A young valet scurried to my car as I ran past him towards the hotel's lobby.

"Sir, I need to give you your ticket," he said with a perplexed look on his face.

"Sorry, kid, I'm in a hurry," I said looking back at him.

Once I was inside the lobby, I went to the elevators that Tiffany and I had used previously. I pressed the upwards button and waited while I caught my breath for a moment. When the elevator arrived, I was the only person going up. I quickly got on and pressed the number twenty-five on the elevator's panel until it lit up.

When I walked off the elevator, I saw Tiffany's condo, front door in the distance, wide open. I then sprinted down the hallway to her residence which was a short distance in front of me. As I got closer, I could hear rumbling going on from inside.

From the front door, I saw Monica and Tiffany locked in each other arms as if they were two pit bulls fighting. The condo was a mess as furniture was overturned and items from the home littered the floor.

"Stop it, Monica!" I yelled out.

Tiffany was the only person that paid attention to my remark as she turned her head towards me. Monica seized the moment by placing both of her hands around Tiffany's neck. With all her strength, she flung Tiffany around onto the glass cocktail table which was in front of the large sofa. The table shattered into pieces as Tiffany's body rested upon it. I was speechless as my eyes expanded to the size of a silver dollar coin. I didn't know my wife possessed that much power in her petite body. Calmly, Monica walked over to Tiffany's body which lay on top of what seemed to be thousands of tiny shards of glass. As she stood over Tiffany's half-dazed body, she simply shook her head in disappointment.

"You pathetic little bitch," Monica said with hatred in her voice. "I'll teach you a lesson or two about messing with my family."

Monica carefully kneeled down next to Tiffany's body and grabbed as much of her long hair as her hand could hold. Then she turned Tiffany's face towards her so she could look into her eyes while she commenced to give her a good old-fashioned ass whipping. Monica took her hand and slapped Tiffany's face firmly. Then she back slapped her quickly. The blows made Tiffany come out of her daze as she frantically tried to escape but Monica had too tight of a grip for that. In all the shock and excitement, Tiffany moved her hand and legs wildly as Monica continued to slap her. The tiny pieces of glass began to cut into her body causing blood to spew out.

"And to think I let your awful ass in my house," Monica yelled out giving another round of blows to Tiffany's face. "Now, my children are dead on count of you!"

"Monica, please stop it!" I shouted out from the front door still amazed at what I witnessed. "You're going to kill her."

"That's what I plan to do, Aaron," Monica said giving me an evil look. Then she went back to delivering the harsh blows on Tiffany's face.

I knew I had to intervene before my wife seriously injured Tiffany. I ran over and bent down trying to pull Monica off her. When I did, Monica wisely elbowed me in my sternum causing me to fall backwards. The impact to my chest knocked the wind out of me momentarily. As I grasped for air, lying on the floor, Monica continued her trouncing of Tiffany. It was as if I had a front-row seat of a heavy weight boxing match. My wife was the prized fighter and she was beating the heck out of her opponent.

"This one is for Brandon you scandalous tramp," Monica said before delivering another hard blow but this time with her closed fist.

"Okay, Monica, please stop," Tiffany sounded off in the agony of defeat.

"I'm not done yet," Monica said raising her fist. "And this one is for Braylon."

The last blow caught Tiffany dead square on her nose and blood poured out immediately. The sight of it seemed to make Monica more deranged as she continued to strike her harder.

"I'm so sorry," Tiffany said faintly beginning to lose consciousness.

"I knew there was something fishy about you when we first met," Monica said pausing for a moment. "You were just too damn friendly for me."

"But it wasn't my idea," Tiffany said hoping to get Monica to stop. "I promise I had nothing to do with it."

"Let her talk, Monica," I said as I was eager to hear what Tiffany had to say.

Monica finally eased up on beating Tiffany's face in. She even let go of Tiffany's hair and her head hit the floor. Then she continued to kneel over her and look on waiting for her to speak.

"He was responsible for it all," Tiffany said beginning to cry as tears fell down her face and mixed with the blood that was on it. "He was the mastermind behind it all. After the accident, I couldn't continue to deal with what just happened."

"Who is he?" Monica asked.

"It was Sebastian," Tiffany answered softly. "We were lovers long before we were friends."

Dismayed and not wanting to believe what Tiffany had just said, Monica and I looked at each other. However, we could clearly tell Tiffany wasn't lying based on the emotional state she was in. She closed her eyes and passed out as her head lay in a small pool of blood.

CHAPTER 22

"Atlanta Police!" shouted two male uniformed officers as they entered Tiffany's condo. They both walked in with a hand on their gun holster being cautious. "Everybody remain calm and stay in your position."

Before they arrived, I had managed to console Monica who was now crying in my arms. We sat near Tiffany's body which was lifeless.

"Officer, there's a woman here who needs medical attention," I said looking over at Tiffany.

One of the officers raced over to Tiffany and felt her wrist for a pulse. He carefully did so being sure he didn't touch any blood on her body.

"She has a faint pulse," said the officer. "I'll call dispatch to send over the paramedics."

"I'm Officer Jackson and that's my partner Officer Crews," said the policeman standing over us. "What's your name?"

"My name is Aaron Malone and this is my wife, Monica," I said. "The woman lying over there is Tiffany Towns."

"Mr. Malone we received a call from Topaz Consulting Group that you were causing a disturbance at their office on Marietta Street," said Officer Jackson looking right at me.

"Officer Jackson, he was only trying to protect me from Tiffany," said Monica speaking up quickly. "I have evidence that will prove she was involved with the deaths of our twin boys."

"Really, Mrs. Malone," said Officer Jackson showing interest. "And what evidence do you have that will show that?"

Monica detached herself from me and unzipped the front pocket of her jogging jacket. She pulled out the DVD Ms. Chastain was referring to and held it up as if it was a key to a treasure chest.

"Here it is, Officer Jackson," said Monica with pride as the sunlight reflected off the DVD in her hand.

"Well, let's just see what you have here," Officer Jackson said taking the DVD from Monica's hand.

He walked over to Tiffany's fifty-two-inch flat screen television mounted on the wall. Then he located the DVD player nearby and turned both electronic devices on. Soon we all were watching the incriminating evidence against Tiffany. The plot to sabotage Monica's Tahoe unfolded right there in front of our eyes. It was too bad Tiffany was still knocked out and wasn't able to see her star performance.

When the viewing of the DVD had ended the paramedics arrived. They were two females wearing rubber gloves and both carried a small medical box.

"We received a call for a request for a paramedic," said one of the women standing in the front door.

"This woman needs your assistance over here," said Officer Crews who was still positioned by Tiffany.

The two women rushed over to where Tiffany was and began to check her vital signs. Everyone was now focused on the outcome of Tiffany's status as we patiently waited.

"It seems as if she is going to be all right," said one of the paramedics. "She just has a slight concussion but she'll be okay."

Tiffany was beginning to come to as her eye lids batted while she looked around. One of the paramedics managed to clean the majority of blood off her that once graced her body. The second paramedic then made her way over to Monica to make sure she was alright.

Officer Jackson walked over to Tiffany as if he was concerned about her safety. He looked down at her as the paramedic helped her sit up.

"Ms. Towns, do you know where you are right now?" he asked.

"Yes, I'm in my condo at the Twelve Hotel," she replied back.

"Ma'am, I just watched some footage of you which may prove you were involved with the deaths of the Malone's twin boys," continued the officer.

"I've already told them it was all Sebastian's plan," Tiffany cried out.

"Ma'am, I'm going to ask you to stand on your feet."

The paramedic helped Tiffany to her feet. She was still groggy but able to stand all by herself.

"Now, place your hands behind your back," ordered Officer Jackson.

"What's going on here, officer?" Tiffany asked.

"You're being arrested for conspiracy to commit murder," he said with force. "You have the right to remain silent. Anything you say can and will be used against you in a court of law. Do you understand?"

"Yes, officer, I understand."

"What's going to happen to her now, officer?" asked Monica as she and I gathered around Tiffany.

"She'll be booked into the Fulton County Jail and held there until her arraignment in front of a judge," he said tightening the handcuffs on Tiffany's wrist.

"What about Sebastian?" Monica asked in an angry tone.

"I'll have one of the detectives at the station issue a warrant for his arrest," he replied. "It may take up to forty-eight hours before a judge signs off on it."

"Forty-eight hours!" I yelled out. "You mean he gets to walk free for that long?"

"Mr. Malone, we have to make sure we follow proper protocol," Officer Jackson stated. "Otherwise, if we arrest him prematurely he could walk on a technicality."

"Well, we both work at the same architect firm called Donaldson and Bradshaw," I said.

"I'll suggest the detectives pick him up there," said Officer Jackson. "We want to preserve the element of surprise. But first things first, let's get Ms. Towns out of here."

By now, the two paramedics had filled out their report, packed their medical boxes, and were headed out the condo. Officer Crews grabbed Tiffany by the arm and proceeded to take her to the squad car located downstairs.

"There's one other thing I failed to mention to you, Monica," Tiffany said before the officer led her out the door.

"What is it, Tiffany?" Monica asked still sounding pissed off.

"I thought about Sebastian the whole time I fucked your husband's brains out," she said with a silly smirk on her face I had seen before.

"Get her out of here!" ordered Officer Jackson as his partner did exactly that.

My heart sank to my feet as I couldn't believe what Tiffany had blurted out. I guess after the beating she took from Monica she wanted to get one final blow in. After the confession, I looked stunned while Monica turned to me.

"Oh my God, Aaron," she said with tears beginning to fill in her eyes. "Is that true?"

"Just wait a minute and let me explain something first," I said.

"Answer me, Aaron!"

FREDERICK GERMAINE

"Monica, it was all a setup," I said trying to get her to understand. "Don't you see it was all part of Sebastian's ploy?"

I moved closer to my wife but she was very apprehensive to accept me. She pushed me away as she gave me a cold stare.

"Get away from me, Aaron."

"Monica, please you just don't understand the full details yet."

"How could you do this to me and tarnish our love for each other?"

"Sweetheart, let me explain everything to you for a second."

"No, I've heard enough of this diabolical plan involving you, Sebastian, and Tiffany," Monica said literally crying now.

"It's not what you think I promise," I said pleading my case to her. "Just calm down so we can go home and talk about it."

"I'm going to calm down alright but not at home with you."

"What?"

"I'm headed home and going to pack a few of my things. Then I'm going over to my parent's house."

"Monica, I think that's a bit premature."

My suggestion was falling on deaf ears as Monica quickly moved towards the front door of the condo. Before she made it there, I tried to stop her but to no avail. She managed to slip her wedding ring off and threw it at me. Then she ended up running down the hallway to an open elevator. Visibly upset, she pressed the down button and was on her way out the hotel.

"Mr. Malone, you may want to let your wife blow some steam off," said Officer Jackson who was still standing there.

I was in the hallway and looked back at him. Then I decided to walk back to where he was. Before I did, I picked up Monica's wedding ring off the floor and placed it in my pocket.

"My wife needs me right now, Officer Jackson."

"I wouldn't doubt that," he said as he pulled a small writing pad from his shirt pocket. "But she also needs time to vent and soak in what just happened. You'll have plenty of time to explain everything to her."

"I feel so guilty and stupid for my actions."

"Hey, don't beat yourself up too bad. We all make mistakes in life."

"Yeah, well probably not like the one I made. It may have cost me my marriage."

"Believe me, Mr. Malone, I've seen worse in my line of work. But for now, I need to find out more about this Sebastian character.

"Well, I would love to get my hands on him right about now."

"Easy, sir, let us do our job and bring him in for questioning the right way."

"Officer Jackson, I just don't know what the motive would be for Sebastian to plot something as destructible as he did."

"So how long have you known, Sebastian?" he asked writing on his pad with an ink pen.

"We met in college and had been the best of friends since."

"Well, sometimes your best friends can be your worst enemies."

"Yeah, I truly believe that now," I said with my head down.

"How about we go downtown to the station where I can continue to ask you more questions?"

"Officer Jackson, I think I really need to go and see about my wife."

"Mr. Malone, it will only take about an hour. Besides, we need to make sure we have enough information on Sebastian so we can bring him in."

"Okay, lead the way," I said giving into his suggestion.

When we made it downstairs, I found the valet and he quickly retrieved my car. Then I followed Officer Jackson's cruiser to the Atlanta Police Department.

At the station, I met a few detectives who wanted to know everything about Sebastian. They asked me a series of questions with some not even pertaining to the case. I ended up staying there a little over an hour. In the end, the detectives assured me they had enough to pick him up once the warrant was signed by the judge. They also asked me not to make contact with him no matter what.

As I drove home back to Sandy Springs, I decided to call Monica at home from my cell phone. I figured she wouldn't pick up the phone and I was absolutely right. The home phone repeatedly rang until it rolled over to voice mail.

Pulling up in the driveway, I could see Monica's car was nowhere in sight. I quickly parked my car and ran inside the house. There in the kitchen, I notice my plate from breakfast still on the table. I turned my attention towards the stairs and yelled out.

"Monica, are you upstairs?" I asked out loud knowing there wouldn't be an answer.

I scampered upstairs to our bedroom and found it the same way as this morning. When I looked in our large walk-in closet, I could tell Monica had taken her suitcase and a lot of her clothes. Missing from the bathroom were all her personal items. Disappointed and dejected, I sat on the end of our bed with my head in my hands. I thought to myself what was I was going to do now.

CHAPTER 23

Two days had passed and I was agitated the police still hadn't picked up Sebastian. The detectives at the police department had assured me the day was coming real soon anytime now. I had made it up in my mind if the police didn't deal with him by tomorrow, I would. I wanted answers for what he had done and, more importantly, retribution for the death of my sons.

Meanwhile, over at the Carmichael's residence, Shanna had dropped by early in the afternoon to comfort her close friend. Monica was still angry with me and refused to accept any of my calls.

"Monica, I knew Aaron was going to eventually cheat on you," Shanna said as the women sat in the kitchen. "All men are dogs!"

"He said it was all a set up by Sebastian," Monica said to her friend.

"And you believe that?"

"I don't know what to believe anymore, Shanna."

"Well, I can believe Sebastian was one shady character," Shanna said with a frown. "I never liked him anyway."

"If Aaron couldn't trust his so-called best friend then who can I trust?"

"You can trust me, Monica, because I'm your real friend to the end."

The two women stood up, embraced, and hugged each other as Monica was still emotional from everything that happened. Then they sat back down.

"I really appreciate you for coming over today, Shanna."

"It's no problem, Monica. So have you spoken to Aaron yet?"

"Not since I last saw him at the Twelve Hotel," Monica said sadly. "I just can't bring myself to speak to him right now."

"Well, I know someone you can definitely speak to."

"Who is that, Shanna?"

"A good divorce lawyer," Shanna said looking very serious.

"I don't want to talk about that right now."

"Why shouldn't you, Monica?"

"Because I think you may be jumping the gun on that discussion."

"You have a right to your opinion, but if Aaron was my husband I'd make the call."

"Aaron was and still is a good husband despite what has happened lately," Monica said with confidence. "He was a great father and provider for our sons, too."

Monica's mother, Allison, had entered the kitchen now before Shanna could get another word in. She smiled at her daughter and Shanna also.

"Hi, Mrs. Carmichael," Shanna said speaking first. "How are you doing?"

"Oh, I'm just fine, Shanna," she said. "So what are you two girls talking about in here?"

"Aaron," Monica said quickly looking at her friend.

"Well, don't worry your pretty head over everything that has occurred," Allison said to her daughter. "Everything will eventually work out for the best."

"You sound so optimistic Mrs. Carmichael," Shanna said in a pessimistic tone with doubt in her eyes.

"You have to be, Shanna, when you've been married as long as I have."

"So, do you think Aaron was wrong for what he did?" asked Shanna.

"I'm not saying he was wrong or right. Yet, sometimes you have to look beyond the scope of the situation."

"What do you mean by that, mom?" asked Monica.

"Dear, every so often, you have to judge a man on how his good deeds greatly outweigh his faults," Allison said to her daughter. "Now, how about I whip us up some lunch to eat?"

"That sounds great, mom."

"Yes, Mrs. Carmichael, it surely does," Shanna said agreeing with Monica.

"Monica, your father just called a few minutes ago," Allison said walking over to the refrigerator.

"He did?"

"Yes, he just finished another lecturing class at Emory. He's on his way over and wanted me to make him some lunch."

"So, what does the head chef of the house plan on cooking?" Shanna asked as she looked at Allison.

"I think I'll make chicken Philly cheese steak sandwiches loaded with green bell peppers and onions," said Allison pulling a few contents from the refrigerator. "And a side order of curly fries to go along with it. How does that sound, girls?"

"It sounds very fattening and high in cholesterol, mom."

"Yes, Mrs. Carmichael, we're still on our diet," Shanna said.

Well, one fattening and high-cholesterol meal won't kill you two," Allison said as she dug into the cabinet next to the stove for a large skillet. "Besides, it's one of your father's favorite quick lunch meals, Monica."

"Since I know that now, I wouldn't dare try to argue with you on that one, mom."

"I promise to cook a healthy and well-balanced meal for dinner this evening. Are you staying for dinner too, Shanna?"

"No, I hadn't planned on it, Mrs. Carmichael. And I didn't want to impose on your family dinner anyway."

"Oh, it's no trouble at all, Shanna. We would love to have you at our dinner table. It makes room for more interesting conversation."

Allison prepped the food she was about to cook and put her cooking skills to the test. In a short while, the veteran chef had the kitchen smelling good enough to make anyone's taste buds water.

Anxiously waiting for some sort of news or development, I decided to grab my keys and head out the house. I figured if Monica was going to avoid all my phone calls, I had no choice but to go to her. Before I did, I wanted to take her something special. And the first thing that came to my mind was red roses.

As I drove down Roswell Road, I came across a small florist shop. I must have passed it a million times to and from work but never patronized the establishment. I was somewhat of a novice with flowers as Jane always was my go to person for items like that. I zipped my car into the florist parking lot and made my way inside.

"Good afternoon, sir," said the friendly female worker as I entered. She was busy making a lily flower arrangement on the counter she stood by.

"Hello," I quietly said as I looked around the tiny shop. I was the only person there but flowers were displayed everywhere.

"So, what can I help you with today?"

"Um, I'm looking for roses but not just any type."

"Ah, I think I might have what you're looking for indeed."

She moved away from the flower arrangement she was working on and led me towards the rear of the store. There we came upon an exquisite display of beautiful roses. They were many colors including yellow, pink, orange, and even red.

"Wow, these are very nice," I said looking overwhelmed at what was in front of me.

"They're more than nice, sir," she said smiling at my lack of knowledge for roses. "These roses were cultivated all the way in California. We had them delivered here via FedEx this morning."

"They're definitely what I'm looking for."

"So, who are you buying these for?" she asked looking at my wedding band on my finger.

"They're for my wife."

"You must be planning a very special occasion."

"Not really," I answered. "They are going to be more of a peace offering."

"Well, she'll know for sure how special she is to you once she takes a look at these roses," she said. "Notice how the petals are full, round, and larger than your normal traditional rose."

"Yes, they are very impressive."

" How many would you like today, sir?"

"I'll take a dozen of the red ones."

She carefully picked out twelve roses and we returned back to the counter where she was when I first came in. There she cut down the roses' stem and thorns. She did all this while handling them as if they were precious as a newborn baby. When she was finished making a few minor adjustments to the roses' appearance, she wrapped them in a delicate colored paper material. Only the rose buds would be displayed as the stems were hidden well inside the paper. Then she placed an elegant bow around them before handing the rose display to me.

"They look perfect," I said with a cheerful smile. "Thanks for all your help."

"No problem at all," she said with an even bigger smile. "I hope she enjoys them."

I paid for the roses and exited the florist shop. When I reached my car, I lay the rose display on the back seat so they wouldn't be damaged. Then I headed for Monica's parents house.

I saw Dr. Carmichael's car in the driveway as I pulled up. He was the last person I wanted to see because I still remembered the conversation we had in Hawaii. I swallowed my pride, grabbed the extraordinary roses, and walked to the front door.

"Sounds like I heard a car door slam outside," said Dr. Carmichael before he stuffed his mouth with the sandwich his wife prepared for him.

His wife, daughter, and even Shanna looked at him baffled as they dug into their lunch at the kitchen table. Allison decided to see if her husband was right and stood up from the table. She made her way to the window in the kitchen that overlooked the driveway.

"You're right, William, it is Aaron who just pulled up."

"He has some nerve coming over here unannounced," said Shanna attempting to instigate the situation.

Monica said nothing and nibbled on her curly fries on her plate. Then she took a sip of ice tea from her glass.

"Excuse me everyone," said Dr. Carmichael standing up from his seat at the table. "I'll handle this."

He rapidly walked to the front door and opened it before I had a chance to ring the doorbell. When I saw him I stood there clutching the roses with a frog in my throat.

"Aaron, it's a surprise to see you."

"Yes, Dr. Carmichael, I'm here to see Monica."

"Cultivated roses, I see you've made an excellent choice."

"Yes sir."

"Well, how about you and I go take a drive?" he said stepping outside and closing the door behind him.

"Sure, Dr. Carmichael," I said nervously. "But what about these roses I brought for Monica?"

"Bring them along, Aaron."

We moved down the walkway that led to the driveway. I noticed he was neatly dressed as usual.

"So, should I drive?" I asked once we reached our vehicles.

"I would prefer you did," he said. "The traffic in Atlanta can be so unsettling for me."

I placed the roses carefully on the back seat as before and we began our unknown departure. The only words he said during our ride were what road to travel and where to turn. I remained silent and hesitated to start a conversation. After a while, we ended up at a golf driving range on North Druid Hills Road.

"So, how's your golf game?" he asked opening his door after I parked.

"It's pretty bad," I said feeling a little more comfortable. "I've been neglecting it a lot lately."

"Now's the perfect time for you to catch up on it," he said. I come here and practice all the time plus it relieves stress.

We walked in together and both received a framed bucket filled with golf balls and a golf club. The interior of the range had individual tee stations where one could stand and hit countless balls into the green which stretched for a couple of hundred yards. The green was littered with balls from previous users. I found an empty tee station and Dr. Carmichael found one right next to me.

"Do you love her, Aaron?" he asked catching me off guard as he placed a golf ball on the tee in front of him.

"Yes, with all my heart, Dr. Carmichael."

"How did the infidelity situation come about?" he asked swinging his club and sending the golf ball out into the green.

"I guess I wasn't thinking with the right head on that fateful night."

"You're young, Aaron, and sometimes with that comes pitfalls you may not be aware of," he said striking another golf ball off his tee. "During your maturation in marriage you have to find a way to side step those pitfalls or they will destroy you."

"Yeah, I see your point," I said as he began to tee up again.

"Remember what I told you I had never done in my marriage back on your wedding day in Hawaii?"

"You said you never…"

"Yes, Aaron, I remember what I said," he announced cutting me off quickly. "But that wasn't the wholehearted truth."

"So, did she ever find out?"

"Oh, yeah, and it did damn nearly killed our marriage," he said sounding ashamed of his past. "It took a long time before she could restore her trust and faith in me but thirty years later we are still together. What I'm trying to say, Aaron, is sometimes negative things happen to make you stronger in the long run."

"I never thought I'd be hearing this from you, Dr. Carmichael."

"I'm telling you this, Aaron, because I want your marriage to succeed like mine despite what has happened. You're going to have to allow Monica to trust you again. It's a gradual process but it can happen."

"Dr. Carmichael, why are you sharing these words of wisdom with me, now?"

"It's because I love my daughter and don't want to see her hurt anymore. Now, are you going to stand there all day and watch me?"

I felt some sort of relief as I grabbed a golf ball out of my bucket and teed off. My shot was horrible as I sliced the ball to the far right.

"That was downright awful, Aaron," said Dr. Carmichael. "You definitely need to practice. Well, tee up again and have another go at it."

We spent the next few hours on the driving range talking as Dr. Carmichael gave me some pointers about my golf game and life in general. I felt we bonded more during our time there than we ever did in the past.

The sun began to set and the rush-hour traffic had picked up when we left the driving range. As I pulled into the Carmichael's driveway for the second time that day, I felt a sense of urgency to speak with Monica but I was nervous.

"Why don't you grab those pretty roses and come on in, Aaron," Dr. Carmichael said as I turned the car's engine off. "You can talk to Monica after we all have dinner together."

"Um, Dr. Carmichael, I think the dinner may be a little extreme right now," I said as I retrieved the roses from the back seat. "I just wanted to talk with Monica one-on-one."

"And you can, in my study, but only after dinner. Besides, the dinner table historically has always been a place for great therapy."

As I walked up the front door with him, I wiped my sweaty forehead. The sweet smell of dinner filled the air as we walked into the house. I was glad he had made the dinner suggestion now. After dinner, I would finally be able to talk to my wife whom I had so desperately waited for.

CHAPTER 24

"Oh, that was so fulfilling, Sebastian, the way you made me come," said Darlene after she just finished riding him. She lay down on his muscular chest breathing heavy with her legs spread between his waist.

"That's good for you but I still want to come too," he said easing his fingertips down her spine.

She pops up and places both hands on his chest looking down into his eyes. Carefully, she balances herself on him so he would remain inside her.

"Why haven't you come yet?"

"Because I aim to please you first, Darlene"

"Sebastian, you've been fucking me all morning and I need to go before Bradley gets home."

"What time is it?" he asked but really not caring.

She looks over to the night stand next to the bed and reached for her watch. As she did, her perfectly round and full breasts dangled in his face.

"Damn, Sebastian, it's already six o'clock in the morning," she said with a slight bit of panic in her voice. "He always gets home by seven."

"Don't worry you'll make it," he said as his tongue began to caress her nipples.

"You're turning me on again licking me like that, Sebastian," she said closing her eyes and tossing her watch away.

"Here is the master plan," he said after pausing from licking her breasts. "Are you listening?"

"Yes," she moaned out with her eyes still closed as she began to gyrate on him.

"When you get home take a quick shower, place a robe on, and roll in the bed as if you had slept there all night. Then, run to the kitchen and fix him a simple breakfast like eggs and toast."

"I understand that's pretty easy," she said in a sultry voice with her eyes still closed. "But what if he wants some?"

"Tell him it's that time of the month for you and enlighten him with a blow job. I guarantee he'll fall asleep like a baby."

"You think that will actually work?"

"I promise it will," he said after he licked her nipples again. "All men fall asleep after they come especially when their bellies are full."

Sebastian had now placed his fingertips on her back again. Although this time, he slowly moved them down her side until he had a firm grip on her ass. She was already riding him pretty steady by now. He lifted her up by her ass making sure his dick was extending all the way in and out of her.

"Hurry up and come, Sebastian, before I get into trouble."

"That's it right there," he said feeling a sense of pleasure. "I'll come when I'm ready to."

"But you're making my pussy sore."

Sebastian didn't care as he gripped her ass harder and pounded deeper into her. Sweat began to permeate through both of their bodies.

"I'm almost there!" he yelled out. "Don't stop riding me."

"I won't, Sebastian," she said clawing her fingers into his back. As she did she leveraged herself perfectly on him. She was in control now riding him even faster. "Let it go, baby!"

"Ah, here it comes!" he exhaled out.

She slowed down her pace a notch but still rode him so he could fully extract himself. After he eased his grip off her ass she knew he was there.

"I want to see you again later tonight, Superman," she said lying on his muscular chest again.

"That shouldn't be a problem," he said laughing and breathing hard.

"Now, I really have to go because he is going to kill me if I'm not there."

"Not before you give me a kiss."

She lifts her head off his chest and obeys his command. Then she springs off his dick, gathers her clothes, finds her watch, and rushes to the bathroom. Within two minutes, she was completely dressed and headed out the front door.

Sebastian stayed up after Darlene left his place and turned on the television to watch a live episode of *Good Morning America*. Before the show came on, he fixed himself a cup of hot tea. The early rays of sunlight beamed through his coverless enormous windows of his loft located on the historic side of the West End district. For the next few minutes, he finished off his tea while sitting in front of the television. Then he made his way to the bathroom where he used a straight razor for his morning shave. He hated having any facial hair so the process of shaving was always quick and easy. A long hot shower washed away any evidence and residue he had just slept with another man's woman. He decided to put on his charcoal grey suit for the lengthy day that awaited him at Donaldson and Bradshaw.

Driving through the downtown connector on his way to work, he punched the accelerator as his Chevy Camaro zipped past the cars on the interstate. He didn't mind the long commute or dealing with traffic as it was a pleasure riding in his new car. Although he contemplated on buying a luxury European sedan, he knew now he had made the right selection.

By nine o'clock, he had made it to his destination and parked his high-performance car in his reserved parking spot. As he entered the building, a friendly voice called out to him.

"Good morning, Mr. Carter."

"Morning to you too, Harold," Sebastian said in a hurry as Harold was shining a pair of shoes for a customer.

"How about a nice shine on those expensive wingtips you're wearing?"

"Maybe during my lunch hour I'll come down and see you," Sebastian said continuing to walk towards the elevators.

"Okay, Mr. Carter, I'll be looking out for you," Harold said with a smile. "Have a good day."

"You do the same, Harold."

The next person Sebastian encountered was the friendly and attractive concierge whose desk was next to the elevators. There were a small group of people waiting for the stainless steel doors to open. He decided on making small talk with the concierge while he waited.

"Well, you're looking quite impressive today," he said flirting with her.

"Good morning to you as well, Mr. Carter," she said as if she was bothered by his advances.

"So, have you given any thought about going to dinner with me?"

"You know it's against my company's policy to fraternize with workers in the building."

"Oh, come on now, I won't tell a soul," he said leaning on her sleek desk. "Besides, it's just a harmless dinner encounter."

"Mr. Carter, I have to follow the rules."

"But sometimes rules are meant to be broken."

The elevator's doors finally opened as the small group of people slowly began to make their way on it. The concierge was relieved as well.

"Looks like your elevator has finally arrived," she said looking at the people behind Sebastian. "Better hurry before you miss it."

Sebastian looked back at the elevator and noticed the last person in the small group getting on. Then he turned to her again.

"Yeah, I see," he said calmly. "Well, think about my proposal, anyway."

"Okay, I'll give it some thought."

Sebastian smoothly moved away from her desk and jumped in the elevator just before the doors closed. He smiled the entire time as the elevator traveled upwards.

Once inside the confinement of Donaldson and Bradshaw, he made his way to his small office. While he traveled there, he stopped at a few of his female colleague's desk to say hi. Inside his office, he took off his jacket and placed it on the back of his chair at his desk. Then he sat down and looked at the phone in front of him. Before he could pick up the receiver in walks a visitor to his office.

"Sebastian, I was making my routine walk throughout the office this morning and thought I'd stop by."

"Good morning, Mr. Bradshaw," said Sebastian quickly standing up in attention as if he was about to salute his boss. "How's everything going this morning?"

"Just fine, Sebastian," he said in a stern tone. "And how are things going with you?"

"It couldn't be any better, sir."

"That's great to hear, Sebastian. In any event, meet me in my office in one hour."

"Do you want to see me regarding the alterations I made to Aaron's work?"

"Actually, yes, but we can talk more in depth about that in an hour," said Mr. Bradshaw as he noticed Sebastian was a little nervous. "It's not that big of a deal but Mr. Black will be joining us too. I'll see you shortly and don't be late."

"Yes sir."

Mr. Bradshaw turned around and walked out of Sebastian's office. When he got to the door he paused and remembered he had to ask Sebastian something else.

"Oh, by the way, how is Aaron doing?"

"I haven't spoken with him lately but I'm sure he is okay," Sebastian said still standing in attention.

"Well, if you speak to him let him know I asked about him. I'll probably have my secretary call him in a few days."

Mr. Bradshaw turned back around and walked away as Sebastian sat down. He refocused his attention to the phone, picked up the receiver, and began dialing. There was a sweet voice on the other end that finally spoke.

"Topaz Consulting Group, how may I direct your call?"

"Yes, I am trying to reach Tiffany Towns, please."

"Sir, Ms. Towns is not in the office at this moment," said the same receptionist I had dealt with a few days ago. "Would you like me to transfer you to her voicemail?"

"Actually, no, I've already left her a few messages."

"If you're one of her clients you may want to try her cell phone."

"Yeah, I've done that too but been unsuccessful, he said twiddling his fingers on his desk. "Maybe I'll just call back later."

After he hung up the phone, he wondered where Tiffany could be. It had now been three days and she failed to return any of his calls. He thought about how uncharacteristic her behavior was. Something must definitely be wrong. He tried to put the pieces of the puzzle together but couldn't find the solution. Before he knew it, time had elapsed and he needed to meet with Mr. Bradshaw.

CHAPTER 25

Dinner with the Carmichael's went well yesterday despite the fact I had to listen to Shanna sarcastic mouth. It was clear she didn't like Sebastian and now I was on her short list. Misery loves company and I guess in her case she didn't want my marriage to succeed. The Carmichael's, on the other hand, took a diplomatic stance during dinner.

My talk with Monica was amicable as we were able to sit down like two civil adults and listen to each other concerns. We decided in order for us to fully reconcile a round of marital counseling would be needed first. I didn't argue about that just as long as I had the opportunity to get my marriage back on track. Monica also stated she would come back home but only when she felt more comfortable.

The only thing that kept me from remaining calm this morning was Sebastian. I had been calling the police department religiously for the last few days and still there wasn't a signed warrant. I'd figured I would make good on my promise to myself if there were no result today. I planned to handle him by myself. Nevertheless, before I did, I placed a final call to the Atlanta Police Department. Surprisingly, my call was transferred to a detective who was now assigned to my case.

"Hey, Ron, pick your damn phone," yelled out another detective in the crowded office of the police department. "There's some guy on hold for you on line three."

Ron, also known as Detective Tate, was now in charge of my case. He was the head of the homicide unit in the department and had been for the last ten years. As he walked through the open floor plan office, with rows of desk scattered about, he chewed on a glazed donut. When he strolled up to his desk and looked at his phone, he noticed the line I had been waiting on was still flashing. He picked up the receiver, pressed the number three line, and spoke.

"Detective Tate here," he said real loud over all the noise in the office.

"Yes, Detective Tate, this is Aaron Malone. I was told my case had been transferred to you."

"Ah, Mr. Malone, I'm glad you called," he said as he gulped down his remaining glazed donut. "I was getting ready to contact you. The judge just signed off on the warrant this morning."

"That's great Detective Tate!" I said with excitement. "So where do we go from here?"

"Well, I'm the lead detective in charge and me and a few officers will be picking up Mr. Carter right away."

"He should be working this morning at Donaldson and Bradshaw. It's an architect firm right here in Atlanta."

"Yeah, that's the information we gathered from Officer Jackson already."

"I'm actually off work today and can meet you at the firm."

"Whoa, Mr. Malone," he said quickly. "Just hold onto your horses for a moment. Let the professionals here at the Atlanta Police Department handle the situation."

"But don't you need somebody to help you identify him?"

"We already spoke to Ms. Towns this morning," he said. "She gave us a good description of him and precisely where his office is located."

"So, I'm forced to keep waiting again?"

"Don't worry, Mr. Malone, we are going to get that bastard today, I promise. Nothing turns my stomach more than a child killer."

"Well, that makes the both of us," I said sternly.

"Mr. Malone, I have been doing this for a long time and I just need for you to really stay put while we handle our job," he said in an authoritarian tone. "I'll be sure to call you once I have personally placed the cuffs on him."

"Okay, Detective Tate, whatever you say."

After my conversation with the detective, I took a seat on the sofa and tried to watch the television. I didn't pay any attention to the images or sounds coming from the flat screen in front of me. All I could do was think about Sebastian.

Across the city at Donaldson and Bradshaw, Sebastian had just placed on his jacket and was preparing to leave his office. He fixed his tie and buttoned up his jacket then moved forward. When he was just outside his office, he heard his phone on his desk ring. He turned around, and then paused, knowing he couldn't be late. Afterwards, he continued on to Mr. Bradshaw's office. He made a detour into the men's restroom which was just a few feet from his destination. As he walked in, one of his colleagues was at the sink washing his hands.

"How's it going, Sebastian?"

"Great Tom," he said nonchalantly walking up to a urinal. There he unzipped his pants and began to relieve himself.

"Hey, I heard you were reassigned to the revitalization project," Tom said pulling a few sheets of paper towel from the machine on the wall.

"Yeah, you heard right."

"So, how is the project coming along?"

"I'm meeting with the boss as soon as I leave here to further discuss some issues," Sebastian said as he flushed the urinal and zipped up his pants.

"Well, I'll see you around Sebastian," Tom said as he finished wiping his hands and tossed the paper towels into the trash can.

"See you later, Tom."

Sebastian made his way over to the sink and turned the water on as Tom walked out the restroom. He quickly lathered his hands with liquid soap and rinsed them under the warm flowing water. Then he turned the water off and walked over to the same paper towel machine Tom was using. As he did, his phone rang which was in his front pocket of his slacks.

"Darn it," I thought I put my cell phone on silent," he said to himself wiping his hands with a few sheets of paper towels. "The last thing I need is for my phone to ring while I'm in a meeting with Mr. Bradshaw." After his hands were dry, he retrieved the phone from his pocket and answered it.

"Hello," he answered sounding frustrated.

"Sebastian, thank God I finally reached you!"

"Tiffany?"

"Yes, it's me."

"Where the hell have you been for the last three days?" he shouted through the phone. "I've been calling you left and right."

"Thank goodness, they haven't gotten to you yet."

"Who are you talking about, Tiffany?"

"I'm talking about the police, Sebastian."

There was a pause of silence as neither one of the two said a word for a few seconds. Sebastian knew his house of cards was beginning to crumble down.

"Where are you, Tiffany?"

"I've been at the Fulton County Jail for the last seventy-two hours," she said sounding defeated. "They know everything."

"You told them?"

"I didn't have a choice, baby," she said beginning to cry. "The Malone's neighbor had evidence of our plan from a security camera. Where are you, now?"

"I'm at the office."

"Get out of there, now!" she frantically said. "The police are on their way. I would have warned you sooner but they just allowed me to use the phone."

"No, Tiffany, tell me it's not true!"

"Listen to me, Sebastian," she said still crying. "I really didn't want it to turn out this way but I still love you."

Crushed his plan had gone awry, Sebastian hung up the phone with Tiffany. He didn't know if the police were listening in on the call or not. Slowly, he walked to the bathroom door and opened it to a slight crack. Through the crack, he looked towards his office and saw a few policemen standing in front of it. Then as he looked in the opposite direction, he saw Detective Tate talking with Mr. Bradshaw right outside his office door.

Sebastian knew he was screwed but had to think fast if he wanted to evade capture. He thought about the exit door near the bathroom which led to the stairwell. His best option was getting to the ground floor.

He closed the slightly cracked bathroom door. Then he took off his tie and jacket and ditched them into the bathroom trash can. He hyped himself up as if he was back on the football field at Florida State and prepared to run. Easily, he made his way down the hall walking fast to the exit door trying not to get noticed. Before he arrived at the stairwell door, a voice shouted out.

"There he is!" shouted Mr. Bradshaw pointing to Sebastian.

"Stop right there, Sebastian Carter!" yelled out Detective Tate as he ran towards the stairwell door. The officers near Sebastian's office soon followed.

Luckily, Sebastian made it inside the stairwell. Then he noticed a fire extinguisher and axe inside a glass case next to the door. He kicked the glass in and grabbed the slender axe. The axe fitted perfectly wedging into the door's handle. Now, the detective and officers on the other side couldn't enter the stairwell.

"He's in the stairwell on the thirty-second floor," Detective Tate said into his walkie-talkie after he unsuccessfully tried to open the door. "Seal off the perimeter and send officers into the stairwell from the floor beneath us."

As soon as Detective Tate barked out his command, a siege of officers came bolting up the stairs towards Sebastian. He only had a split second to think and knew right then his sole option was the roof which was two floors up. Before he moved, he took the fire extinguisher and sprayed the white powdery fog on the officers below. This camouflage gave him some extra time as the officers had to be cautious.

When he reached the door to the roof, it was jammed but he used his brute strength and powered it open. He looked behind him and saw the officers racing up the stairs. Wisely, he kicked off the inside door handle. By doing this, the door would lock and couldn't be open. He smiled as he knew he was inches away from permanently disappearing.

Sebastian walked out on the enormous roof and quickly turned around and slammed the door behind him. It was just in the nick of time as an avalanche of officers, on the other side of the door, were kicking and pounding it with no results. He gathered himself, took a second to breathe, and then turned around facing the roof again. When he did there was a huge surprise waiting for him.

"Take that you son-of-a-bitch!" I exclaimed as I punched him in his nose. "There was no way I'd let the police get a hold of you before I did."

Being the smart and savvy designer whom I was, I sat around all morning putting myself in Sebastian's shoes. I figured the roof would be his only viable option once he knew the police were on to him. My ingenious plan had now paid off and it was time for payback.

"Aaron, you mother fucker!" he yelled back at me bending down holding his nose as blood poured onto his hands. "I think you just broke my nose."

"That's not all I'm going to break."

Sebastian took his hands down from his face and wiped the blood on his expensive shirt. I could see the hate in his eyes as he charged me like a mad bull. When he reached me, our bodies interlocked like two wrestlers as we fell down on the roof. Still intertwined, we rolled around over each with each man trying to gain the better position. I was finally able to maneuver myself on top of him.

"You damn asshole, why did you do it?" I asked and then punched him repeatedly in the nose. I was trying to take his nose off his face as blood was going everywhere by now. "Why did you have to kill my twin boys?"

Before he could answer there was a loud thunderous sound approaching above us and the wind was picking up immensely. I looked up and there was a massive helicopter hovering on top of us.

"What the hell is this?" I said looking into the sky as I stopped pounding in Sebastian's face.

"This is the Atlanta Police Department," said an officer from the helicopter's siren system. "You're surrounded with nowhere to escape. Get faced down on the roof, now!"

Sebastian took this opportunity and sucker punched me. He caught me squarely on my chin and the blow knocked me backwards. Then he jumped on top of me and punched my right eye twice as my head bounced off the roof. He was too strong and powerful for me to overtake.

"You never would understand anyway, Aaron," he said as he raised his fist again attempting to deliver another harsh blow. Suddenly, he paused, looked at me, and then spat in my face. "I never did like your geeky ass anyway." Then instead of finishing me off, he rose to his feet and took off running on the roof.

"Subject, get down now!" ordered the officer from the helicopter.

Sebastian didn't comply but kept running to the center of the roof. I figured he planned to take cover near the large air compressors. In front of the compressors was the even larger skylight. The pilot swooped down closer to Sebastian running as the wind kicked up more now. Then the officer in the helicopter let off a warning shot. It must have scared the heck out of Sebastian because he eventually slipped, lost his balance, and fell onto the skylight before he could reach the compressors. As he did, the glass shattered and I saw him disappear.

Still in shock from the blows he had given me with my right eye almost swollen shut, I picked myself up and rushed over to the skylight. There in front of me, I saw him hanging barley onto a piece of metal as his body dangled above the thirty-four floors beneath him. I could see the glass had already made it down to the lobby underneath him. The people below were amazed at what they were witnessing above them. He continued to dangle looking at me too prideful to ask for my help.

"I'm not going to let you get off that easy," I said as I bent down and grabbed his forearm. "You're going to rot in prison first and then hell."

Instinctively, he attached his other hand to my assisting arm as I tried to pull him up. The wind from the helicopter's blades wasn't making the task any easier. Then I felt him purposely letting his grip go.

"No, Sebastian, don't do it!"

"It's better this way, Aaron."

"Why did you have to do it?" I screamed over the helicopter's noise still hovering above us.

"You'll never understand," he said looking aimlessly into my eyes as he let go.

I stared back into his eyes until his body splattered like a tomato on the lobby floor. As I continued to look downwards, the crowd below was in a full panic by now. People everywhere were running and screaming wildly. I even got a glimpse of Harold staring up at me as if he couldn't believe what just happened. I was beyond disappointed because the man who had all the answers to my questions was dead now.

CHAPTER 26

The day after Sebastian's untimely death, Tiffany's arraignment finally came up. With my swollen right eye, I met Monica and her parents at the Fulton County Courthouse located on Pryor Street in downtown Atlanta. We were all overly anxious to hear and see what sort of results would occur today.

As all four of us sat on the front bench in the courtroom, I noticed it was a few minutes past ten o'clock in the morning based on the clock on the wall in front of me. There were only a handful of people in the quiet courtroom with us. Standing next to the door, where the judge would enter, stood a bailiff dressed in a neatly pressed uniform. He stared straight, showed no emotions, and seemed liked he had been lifting weights his entire life.

In front of the judge's bench there were two tables. At one table sat Paula Hollandale the experienced district attorney who had prosecuted hundreds, if not thousands, of cases for Fulton County. She sat there professionally dressed and was scribbling on her notepad. To the table next to her sat a man who was the public defender. He seemed as if he forgot to shave this morning and wore a cheap suit. I could tell he had been overburden with work as there was a stack of files on the table next to him where he sat. After a few more people made their way inside the courtroom, we all finally heard a distinctive command.

"All rise," announced the bailiff really loud to the small audience. "The Honorable Judge Johnson J. Morton now presiding."

On cue, everyone in the courtroom stood up as the judge entered and made his presence. He was a tall black man with a bald head. His black robe fitted him perfectly as he kept a serious demeanor on his face walking to his chair behind his bench. He was known as one of the harsher judges that didn't allow too much room for leniency in his courtroom.

"You may be seated," he said firmly as he sat down in his chair. "Bailiff, call the first case."

"Docket number 3256783, the State of Georgia versus Tiffany Towns," he said as he read from a folder in his hand.

After the bailiff read the introduction for the first case, he walked over to the judge and handed him the folder he had just read from. While the judge reviewed the contents of the folder, two female sheriff deputies escorted Tiffany into the courtroom. She was looking awful as ever wearing a red jumpsuit, no makeup, and her hair hadn't been combed in days. The sheriff deputies led her to the male public defender that was now standing up at his table. Even the district attorney had stood up waiting to hear the first words from the judge.

"Ms. Towns, it's my understanding you have been unable to retain an attorney," said Judge Morton looking at her. "Thus, the court has provided one for you. Is this correct?"

Before Tiffany could agree to what Judge Morton asked her, the courtroom swinging doors in the rear burst open. In walked a woman carrying a leather case containing what seemed to be a legal file.

"No, it's not your Honor," yelled out the dainty, yet fashionable, woman strolling up to Judge Morton's bench.

"Hey, that's Katrina Hope, the high profile defense attorney," said a man out loud to his friend sitting at a bench near us. "I just saw her on *TMZ* the other day."

As the small crowd finally figured out who the sophisticated woman was, plenty of noise quickly filled the once-so-quiet courtroom.

"Order in the court!" shouted Judge Morton as he struck his gavel.

"Your Honor, I was retained by Sebastian Carter prior to his unfortunate death to represent the interest of Ms. Towns," said Katrina in front of the judge's bench. "I actually just filed my letter of representation with the court this morning."

Katrina handed Judge Morton a document to read. As he overlooks the document, the courtroom looks stunned and waits patiently.

"Well, Ms. Hope, it's so wonderful to finally see you again in my courtroom," said Judge Morton sarcastically. "I'll duly note your representation of Ms. Towns. You may take your position by your client."

"It's always a pleasure to see you too, your Honor," said Katrina before she walked over to the defense table. As she did the courtroom erupted with more noise.

"Order in the court!" barked out Judge Morton again as he struck his gavel for a second time.

Katrina Hope wasn't just any ordinary attorney, she was best money could buy. She was a partner at the prestigious law firm McLaughlin, Hope, Berkowitz and Lee headquartered in downtown Atlanta. Her firm handled defending high profile celebrity criminal cases and corporate civil claims. Her clients often were acquitted on a regular basis. As she stood next to Tiffany, she was dressed exclusively for the day. I wasn't a fashion guru but I noticed her wardrobe had a bit of flair to it, including her designer red-bottom heels.

It was now time for Judge Morton to read the charges the state had brought against Tiffany. As he prepared to do so, Katrina stood by her client and whispered in her ear. The public defender has now moved away from the table and sat on another bench near us.

"Ms. Towns, you are being charged with," started Judge Morton but Katrina quickly cut him off.

"Your Honor, we object to the reading of the formal charges," said Katrina.

"I won't allow it in my courtroom, counselor."

"But, your Honor, we have a right not to have the formal charges read out loud," said Katrina sounding upset and protesting.

"Yes, Ms. Hope, I understand that. However, as you may know, I always read the defendant's formal charges out in my courtroom."

"Yes, your Honor."

The district attorney smiled at Judge Morton's comment then she looked at Katrina and rolled her eyes. It was obvious she wasn't too fond of her legal opponent or her tactics.

"Now, as I was saying," Judge Morton said. "Ms. Towns you're charged with two counts of conspiracy to commit murder for the deaths of Brandon and Braylon Malone. Additionally, you are also charged with one count of attempted murder for Monica Malone. How do you wish to plea?"

"My client wishes to plead not guilty, your Honor," said Katrina proudly.

That comment from Katrina must have struck a nerve with Monica who was sitting next to me. Before anyone knew it, she stood up and let out a cry.

"You murdered my sons, you pitiful witch!" Monica said in an outburst while standing up.

"Monica, it's going to be okay," I said quickly standing to my feet and grabbed onto her. "Let the judicial system handle it."

"Order in the court!" cried out Judge Morton slamming down his gavel. It was evident he was becoming visibly upset by now. "Young lady not another word out of your mouth or I'll hold you in contempt. Do I make myself absolutely clear?"

"Yes sir," Monica said softly and we both sat down.

"Your Honor, the defense would like to file a motion to suppress the state's evidence," said Katrina. She then reached into her leather case and pulled out a miniature manuscript of paperwork.

"And what evidence do you wish to suppress, Ms. Hope?" asked Judge Morton.

"My client's statement to the arresting officer and the DVD the state plans to show as evidence," replied Katrina.

Katrina then asked for permission to approach the bench and same was granted. Once in front of Judge Morton, she handed him her paperwork which included her motion. He quickly reviewed the documents as she walked back to the defense table.

"Your Honor, we will gladly file an objection to the defense motion to suppress evidence," said Paula Hollandale, the district attorney, finally speaking up.

"Yes, Ms. Hollandale, I anticipated that response from you," said Judge Morton still looking at the paperwork from Katrina. "File your objection within seventy-two hours and I'll make a determination."

"Yes, your Honor," said the district attorney.

"Now, in the matter of bail, I would like to hear the recommendation from the state first," said Judge Morton looking at the district attorney.

"Your Honor, the state's position is that we adamantly and vehemently request the defendant remain in custody without bail," said the district attorney looking at Tiffany. "We base our suggestion on the fact the crime was heinous in nature and with intent. Furthermore, we believe the defendant poses a potential flight risk."

"The defense objects, your Honor," said Katrina giving the district attorney a harsh stare. "My client is completely innocent and the evidence will show likewise. The defense plans to show this at trial and fully exonerate Ms. Towns. Also, Ms. Towns, is gainfully employed, respected in the community, and has family ties right here in Atlanta."

"Ms. Hope, please save the theatrics for the actual trial," said Judge Morton. "This is clearly just an arraignment hearing. As for now, bail is denied."

Slightly rejected, but not quite defeated, Katrina still had one legal strategy up her sleeve. She stood poised and began to speak again.

"Your Honor, there is one other issue the defense would like to address."

"Yes, Ms. Hope, let me guess," said Judge Morton with a smile. "You'd like to request for a change in venue."

"Absolutely, your Honor."

"Well, let me save you the time and effort of filing your motion because I'm denying that too."

Katrina looked hot and bothered as she knew she would have a strict battle with Judge Morton once the trial got underway. Now, the district attorney was smiling even more than before. Judge Morton finally struck his gavel for the last time and asked the bailiff to announce the next case.

CHAPTER 27

It had now been a few days since we were in the courtroom but everything still lingered on my mind. I was disappointed at what had transpired at Tiffany's arraignment even though the judge denied her bail. After talking with the district attorney in length that day, she advised us the trial would likely occur in two years. So that meant for the next few years Monica and I had to continue to live with the pain of our son's death without any closure.

On a positive note for today, I was actually headed back to work this morning. Mr. Bradshaw's secretary had called me and made me aware I was now permanently assigned to the revitalization project. I was anxious at getting back to work even though the King and Queen Towers had been engulfed in a media frenzy since Sebastian's death. The occurrence made the front page of the *Atlanta Journal Constitution* and even *CNN* had set up a live broadcast remote from the building. All of this was the wrong attention Mr. Bradshaw wanted for his company. Thus, he hired a big-shot public relations firm to come in and help restore his company's clean-cut image. The last thing he wanted was his investors pulling out of the revitalization project.

As I headed out the house, I had gotten acclimated to not smelling breakfast cooking in the kitchen or the constant noise from the twins. I so desperately wanted my wife back in our home but cherished to hold and hug my boys even more. The thought of finally going back to work would hopefully cheer me up.

When I walked through the building's lobby doors, there was Harold smiling as always. He was occupied shining a pair of shoes for a man seated in one of his chairs. The man was busy reading his morning newspaper as Harold paused for a moment to speak to me.

"It's great to see you back again, Mr. Malone," Harold said with enthusiasm as I stopped in front of his work area.

"Thank you, Harold. It's great to be back at work again."

"It was so sad to have witnessed how everything turned out with Sebastian, Mr. Malone. I didn't even see that coming."

"None of us did, Harold. Even so, I figured in the end he got what was coming to him."

"I guess you're right."

"Hey, these loafers I'm wearing could use a patented shine from you," I said looking down at my shoes.

"It would be all my pleasure, Mr. Malone."

"Okay, Harold, I'll come back downstairs later today."

"See you then, sir," he said and went back to finishing up his customer.

Before I walked over to the elevators, I strolled to the middle of the lobby. I noticed the sunlight still beamed eloquently through the replaced skylight. Even the marble tiles had been repaired professionally. I looked upwards to the skylight and then back down. It was as if the incident with Sebastian had never even happened. I stepped away, walked to the elevators, smiled at the concierge, and then traveled upstairs.

The familiarity of the large double glass doors etched with Donaldson and Bradshaw was a great sight to see as I walked off the elevator. As soon as I walked in, all the employees noticed and began to clap and cheer as if I was receiving a hero's welcome. Even Mr. Bradshaw was there smiling too and greeted me with a firm handshake. Then the two of us retired to his office where he brought me up-to-date on the revitalization project and all his efforts with the public relations firm.

After talking with Mr. Bradshaw for over an hour, it was back to business as usual and I was glad of it. Walking back to my office, everyone I passed gave me a congratulatory handshake or hug. However, the most important person waiting for me was Jane. When I arrived at my office, she was standing in the doorway smiling as if she was my grandmother and gave me the biggest hug ever.

"Oh, Mr. Malone, we all are so proud of you," she said after hugging me. "And I'm glad you finally returned back to work."

"Me too, Jane," I said as we both stood in the doorway to my office. "I was actually losing my mind at home all day."

"So how is Mrs. Malone doing?"

"She's doing much better."

"Well, that's great to hear, Mr. Malone."

"So have you been holding down the fort since I've been gone?"

"Very much so but I was becoming anxious on when you would be returning," she said blushing a bit. "Oh, I almost forgot, let me give you something."

As Jane went over to her desk, I realized she definitely was someone you would only meet once in a lifetime. Her authenticity for being a true loving human being was something few could compare to.

"And this package is for you," she said handing me a medium sized white envelope which was sealed.

"What is this, Jane, some sort of present?" I asked looking bewildered at the envelope as I took possession of it.

"No, Mr. Malone, it's the idea I came up with for your fifth-year wedding anniversary," she said. "Remember, you said we would talk about it a few months ago but it never happened."

"Jane, you're a lifesaver," I said then gave her a hug. "Can you believe I failed to realize our wedding anniversary is in less than two weeks?"

"You've been under a lot of stress that would cause anyone to forget that."

"Well, let's see what's inside the envelope," I said about to tear it open.

"No, Mr. Malone, you can't," she said stopping me. "It's supposed to be a surprise. Just wait and open it up with your wife tonight."

Jane was unaware Monica was staying at her parent's house while we tried to rehabilitate our marriage. So I figured I wouldn't tell her otherwise.

"Okay, I'll do that, Jane. By the way, thanks for everything."

We ended our conversation and I headed into my office. Everything was still in place as I left it. Of course, the view from my office was as magnificent as always with the bottleneck traffic on the interstate. I worked diligently throughout the day but had enough time to break away and let Harold put a spit shine on my loafers. Before I knew it, seven o'clock had arrived and it was time to go home for the day. Jane and everyone else had left the office long ago. I guess working late didn't bother me because I didn't want to go home to an empty house. I grabbed my jacket, the white envelope from Jane, and headed home.

When I arrived home, I didn't even bother to park inside the garage but rather in the driveway. I figured the morning would arrive soon enough and it really didn't matter where my car rested for the night. I strolled up to the front door with my jacket folded over my arm while I fumbled for the house key. As I entered the house, the smell of beef steaks cooking unexpectedly caught my attention. I calmly walked to the kitchen and she was standing there waiting on me.

"Monica?" I said looking astonished.

"Hello Aaron."

I placed my jacket on the arm of the kitchen chair and lay the white envelope on the table. Then I hugged Monica without wanting to let her go.

"Sweetheart, I'm so glad you're home," I said softly into her ear as I continued to hug her. "I missed you, dearly."

"It's good to be back too, Aaron. I missed you."

I finally stopped hugging Monica and we detached but remained close to each other as I held her hand. I thought about the white envelope Jane had given me and now would be the perfect time to open it.

"I have a surprise for you, sweetheart," I said as I reached for the white envelope on the kitchen table.

"What type of a surprise could it be?" she asked.

"It pertains to our fifth-year wedding anniversary. But you'll have to close your eyes first."

"Okay, Aaron, whatever you say."

While Monica had her eyes closed, I ripped opened the white envelope and looked at what Jane had given me. I had a big smile on my face. Then I told Monica to open her eyes and her smile was even bigger than mine.

CHAPTER 28

I was elated it was only a few days until Monica and I celebrated our fifth-year anniversary. By no means was our marriage fixed but I was glad of the direction it was headed in. We even had another meeting with our marriage counselor yesterday which I found fulfilling. As I sat at my desk finalizing the revitalization project, Jane called through on my phone's intercom system.

"Mr. Malone, I have an urgent call waiting for you."

"Sure thing, Jane, who is it?"

"The caller said her name is Paula Hollandale."

I immediately stopped working and quickly picked up the phone's receiver and placed it to my ear. I knew it had to be very important if the city's district attorney was calling me.

"Please send her through to my main line, Jane."

"Right away, Mr. Malone."

While I waited for Paula to be connected with me, I swallowed what seemed to be the biggest knot in my throat. Then Jane joined our call.

"Hello, Mr. Malone, this is Paula Hollandale."

"Hi, Ms. Hollandale," I said in a curious tone. "How are things going with you?"

"Oh, pretty much the same, sir. The crimes don't slow down or stop and we continue to prosecute."

"Yeah, I'd image you have your hands full especially in the city of Atlanta."

"Well, having my hands full with cases is a bit of an understatement," she said in a joyous tone. Then we both laughed together at her statement.

"So, what can I do for you this morning, Ms. Hollandale?" I asked turning the conversation to a serious tone.

"I need for you to come right away to my office at the Fulton County Courthouse."

"Why now?"

"Because Ms. Towns is ready to confess," she said. "But this time it's with her world-famous attorney as we record her confession. Ms. Towns stated she wouldn't proceed unless you were present."

"Why does she want me there, Ms. Hollandale?"

"Apparently, Mr. Malone, her conscience is eating her up inside by now. Either that or her attorney is seeking a bit of leniency from the judge at sentencing. After her attorney found out we would be asking for the death penalty at trial, we received a call this morning in regard to a plea deal."

"So, what's the plea deal for Ms. Towns?" I asked.

"Life without the possibility of parole, Mr. Malone," she said with firmness. "I wouldn't strike a deal any other way."

"Okay, I'm going to pick up my wife first and head right over."

"Oh no, Mr. Malone, you can't do that," she said catching me off guard.

"Why not, Ms. Hollandale?"

"Because Ms. Towns gave strict instructions she wouldn't confess if your wife or her parents were in the room with us."

"Well, it seems as if I'm in a delicate situation where I'm compelled to obey," I said back to her. "I'm on my way."

When I arrived at the courthouse, there was a sheriff deputy waiting for me in the lobby. He quickly took me upstairs to the district attorney's office. In the room were Tiffany, Katrina, and a team of lawyers for the prosecutor's office. Tiffany looked withdrawn but relieved all this madness was finally coming to an end. I said nothing and was told to simply sit down and listen as the confession began.

Tiffany told this unimaginable story how she first met Sebastian five years ago at a nightclub here in Atlanta. Back then, she was just in town on some business with her consulting firm. The two hit it off that same night and had been distance lovers ever since.

Apparently, Sebastian put the wheels in motion to his sinister plan the day Monica and I were married. He initially wanted me to eat my words when I said "I would never cheat on my wife." After he met Tiffany, she agreed to help him but only as a practical joke initially.

However, as the years went by and I progressed more at Donaldson and Bradshaw, Sebastian felt shortchanged. He began to hate and envy me and my life. What was even more disturbing was how he claimed to love being a bachelor but adamantly told Tiffany he wanted what I had. Yes, it was the pretty wife, kids, nice cars, suburban home, and continuous advancement at work which he longed for. Somehow, he never was able to achieve or obtain what I had. Jealously trumps greed all day long and Sebastian's deeds proved that.

It was so sad to believe Tiffany got tangled further into his evil plot the more she fell in love with him.

Now, you may have been fooled at the beginning of this story when you thought Tiffany was the ultimate eye candy but you were dead wrong. The eye candy that Sebastian so desperately wanted was me or rather the life I lived.

When I left the courthouse that late afternoon, I felt sick to my stomach. I had all the answers I needed even though I still felt confused not understanding why Sebastian turned out the way he did. I was disappointed in myself for calling him my best friend or even trusting him so much during the time I had known him.

Two days later at the sentencing, I sat in the same courtroom to hear Judge Morton issue a ruling. After he was advised a plea deal had been agreed to, he expedited the sentencing phase. Monica and her parents decided not to attend as they had heard enough of Tiffany and Sebastian's ploy by now. Without any reservations, Judge Morton sentenced Tiffany to prison for the rest of her natural life without parole. Tiffany cried, turned to me, and said she was so sorry for everything. Then the female deputies led her away. Katrina looked sadden as her ego was bruised but only for a split second. Tomorrow, it would be back to the grind in her never-ending litigious world. I shook Ms. Hollandale's hand and graciously thanked her. Then I walked through the swinging doors of the courtroom with mixed emotions and never looked back.

EPILOGUE

THE WEDDING ANNIVERSARY IN HAWAII

SATURDAY, JUNE 30, 2012

Monica and I were back on the island of Kauai, Hawaii, to celebrate our fifth-year anniversary. It had been exactly five years to the date we were married here. We even managed to secure our same honeymoon suite on the resort where we would be staying for the next few days. Nevertheless, I owed it all to Jane as it was her brilliant idea for us to spend our anniversary here. She was able to secure the airline tickets and resort room with my American Express card which she always had access to.

As we walked holding hands on the beach, the white sand felt smooth on our bare feet. The sun was setting and the tide was rising as waves struck our ankles periodically while we continued to walk the coastline. When we reached the white gazebo where we were married just off in the distance, we stopped and marveled at it. Apparently, there was a couple scheduled to tie the nuptials at the same gazebo tomorrow as it was fully decorated. I figured this would be the perfect time to talk to Monica. Bending down on one knee, while continuing to hold her hand, I looked into her eyes and spoke.

"Oh, Aaron, you don't have to do that."

"Just listen to me, Monica, because it's part of my gift to you."

Over last few days, I had been practicing my wedding lines to myself. I wanted my words to flow eloquently without any mistakes as I renewed my vows with my wife. Now, the tide was rising faster as the water raced along my leg as I kneeled in the white sand.

"I Aaron take you, Monica, to be my wife, to have and to hold, from this day forward, for better, for worst, for richer, for poorer, in sickness and in health, to love and to cherish, till death do us part."

Monica was always an emotional person so by now tears of joys were flowing down her pretty face. She held my hand even tighter as I continued.

"I promise to always respect, love, and most importantly never to be unfaithful to you ever again."

Before she could say a word, I pulled her wedding ring out of my pocket. Soon after the incident at the Twelve Hotel, I took her ring and had it professionally cleaned and shined. I even had the jeweler add four more carats to it. Thus, each carat would symbolize a year of our marriage. Now, the five carat wedding ring was even more riveting as I held it up to her. The sun's evening rays shined perfectly through it.

"This wedding ring is a symbol of eternity," I said looking into Monica's eyes with passion. "It is an outward sign of an inward and spiritual bond that unites two hearts in endless love. Furthermore, it is a token of our love and deep desire to be forever united in heart and soul. Monica, I give you this ring as a symbol of my love and faithfulness to you."

I slipped the ring on her finger, rose to my feet, and kissed my wife. Our lips locked for an extended period of time as we hugged each other. Then our lips finally unlocked.

"Aaron, I love you so much and always will," she said with tears still flowing down her face. "I never want our love to ever waver again."

"It won't, sweetheart, I can promise you that," I said as I wiped the tears from her face. "And I love you so much, too. Can you ever forgive me for what I did?"

"Yes, Aaron, I forgave you a long time ago."

I placed my wife's hand in mine as we continued to stroll on the beach with the crystal-clear blue water running over our feet. I guess all marriages go through some sort of test in life. It's how you rebound and are willing to make it work rather than throw it all away. If our marriage had dissipated, then I guess Sebastian would have gotten what he really wanted. It would be a while until he was fully out of our minds, if ever. However, one thing is for certain that I learned from this whole diabolical situation. Be sure you select your friends carefully as they may be taking an opportunity to make you their next "Eye Candy."

The End

ABOUT THE AUTHOR

Frederick Germaine has always been fascinated how writing could be so intriguing. It takes dedication and an imaginable thought process to capture an audience within a good novel. After writing leisurely for years, Frederick Germaine decided to publish his first novel. *Ladies' Man* is an entertaining love novel from a male-perspective. He wrote the novel because he felt almost everyone has previously been in love, is currently in love, or simply seeking love. Thus, we all can relate to it.

After the release of *Ladies' Man* in 2011, Frederick Germaine has been featured in various publications. Additionally, his debut novel has been reviewed and discussed favorably among many book clubs, reviewers, and avid book readers.

In 2012, Frederick Germaine launched his sophomore novel titled *Eye Candy*. Keeping a love and romance theme, this work excitingly thrills an audience with unpredictable suspense.

Frederick Germaine's achievements include being named as a finalist for the coveted 2012 National Black Book Festival Best New Author Award.

Frederick Germaine graduated from Jacksonville State University where he earned a Bachelor's Degree in Business. He currently resides in Atlanta where he continues to write and promises to deliver another hot novel.

For more information on Frederick Germaine please visit his website: www.frederickgermaine.com